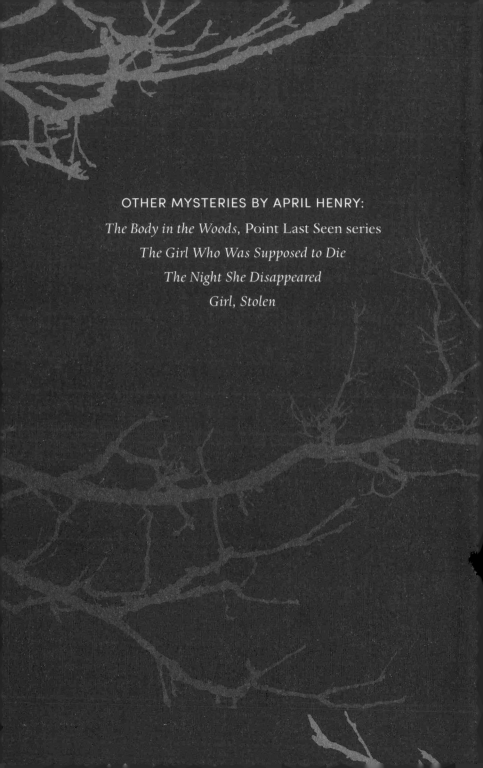

POINT
LAST
SEEN

BLOOD
WILL
TELL

APRIL HENRY

Christy Ottaviano Books

Henry Holt and Company, LLC
Publishers since 1866
175 Fifth Avenue
New York, New York 10010
macteenbooks.com

Library of Congress Cataloging-in-Publication Data
Henry, April.
Blood will tell / April Henry. —First edition.
pages cm.   —(Point last seen ; [2])
"Christy Ottaviano Books."
Summary: "Teen Portland Search and Rescue team member Nick
Walker becomes a prime suspect in a murder"—Provided by publisher.
ISBN 978-0-8050-9853-2 (hardback)—ISBN 978-0-8050-9867-9 (e-book)
[1. Murder—Fiction.   2. Criminal investigation—Fiction.   3. Friendship—
Fiction.   4. Eccentrics and eccentricities—Fiction.   5. Mystery and
detective stories.]   I. Title.
PZ7.H39356Bl 2015   [Fic]—dc23   2014048673

Henry Holt books may be purchased for business or promotional use.
For information on bulk purchases, please contact the Macmillan Corporate
and Premium Sales Department at (800) 221-7945 x5442 or by e-mail
at specialmarkets@macmillan.com.

First Edition—2015

Printed in the United States of America by R. R. Donnelley & Sons Company,
Harrisonburg, Virginia

1 3 5 7 9 10 8 6 4 2

FOR JAKE KELLER,
WHO WOULDN'T LET ME DEDICATE
THE LAST BOOK TO HIM

Whatever [the criminal] touches, whatever he leaves, even unconsciously, will serve as silent evidence against him. Not only his fingerprints or his footprints, but his hair, the fibres from his clothes, the glass he breaks, the tool mark he leaves, the paint he scratches, the blood or semen he deposits or collects—all these and more bear mute witness against him. This is evidence that does not forget. It is not confused by the excitement of the moment. It is not absent because human witnesses are. It is factual evidence. Physical evidence cannot be wrong; it cannot perjure itself; it cannot be wholly absent. . . . Only human failure to find it, study and understand it, can diminish its value.

—Paul Kirk, *Crime Investigation*

BLOOD WILL TELL

CHAPTER 1
NICK
SUNDAY

BLOOD AND BONES

FRESHLY SPILLED BLOOD IS WET, SHINY, and startlingly crimson. Newly exposed bone is a pearly, glowing white.

Blood and bones. Before the night was out, Nick Walker would see things that would drop him to his knees. Before the week was out, he would do things he would have said were impossible. And he would learn truths that he would desperately wish were lies.

A GOOD GIRL

IN A LITTLE OVER AN HOUR, SEVEN-YEAR-OLD Mariana Chavez would be lying in a ditch, her unseeing eyes staring at the stars.

But for now, Mariana lay on her back looking up at the lights on Home Depot's faraway ceiling. She was stretched out on a low, flat cart topped with curved bars that looked like an orange jungle gym. She lifted one of her legs so she could admire her new rain boot, red with black dots. The best part were the toes, decorated with eyes and antennae. The boots looked just like ladybugs.

"Why is this so confusing?" Mariana's mom muttered as she scanned the rows of little round pieces of shiny metal and black rubber that would somehow fix the drippy kitchen faucet. "And why must Mr. Edmonds be so"—she paused and Mariana knew she was skipping over a swear word—"so useless?"

Mr. Edmonds was their apartment manager. He was the one who was supposed to fix things. Only two years ago he had tried to fix the leaking toilet and just made it worse. And after that, Mariana's mom had started just trying to fix anything that broke herself.

Mariana also didn't like Mr. Edmonds, but for different reasons. When her mom wasn't watching, he sometimes stared at her. And said things to her, too, about how pretty she was, about how she seemed older than seven. It wasn't that she minded being told those things. She just didn't like to hear them from Mr. Edmonds, who looked a little like a tanned lizard.

Finally her mom picked something and paid for it. When they drove home, it was already growing dark. Mariana helped carry in the groceries they had bought before going to Home Depot, staggering a little under the weight of the bags.

"You're a good girl, Mariana," her mom said, resting her hand briefly on her shoulder. "You're a good helper."

Helper reminded Mariana of what would come next. Putting away the groceries and then holding a flashlight while her mom swore at the wrench and the faucet and Mr. Edmonds and complained that Mariana wasn't holding the light still.

"Can I go over to Hector's to play?" Hector was her best friend. He lived in the next apartment building.

Her mom was already shaking her head. "I don't think so, honey."

"Please . . ." Mariana drew the word out.

Her mom relented. "Okay. I guess you've earned it."

But when Mariana knocked on the door to Hector's apartment, no one answered. It was fully dark now. She knocked again, but there were no sounds from inside. She was dragging her feet back down the walk, not at all eager to go home and hold the flashlight, when she spotted something that made her stop.

A kitten. A little black-and-gray-striped kitten. It took one startled glance at her and then ran around the corner.

Mariana loved kittens. And if she brought this one home, maybe this time her mom wouldn't say no. Not when it was right there in their apartment and already best friends with Mariana.

Hands outstretched, Mariana ran around the corner and into the darkness.

Ninety minutes later, Mariana's mom called Hector's mom to say it was time for her daughter to come back. And learned that the family had only been home for fifteen minutes—and that they had not seen Mariana.

AGAINST HER WILL

WHEN THE TEXT LIT UP HIS PHONE, NICK was doing his homework. Or, to be more accurate, he had his history textbook open while he watched YouTube music videos on his laptop.

911 Assist near Gresham—Missing 7 yo—
Meet @ 2100

The text was from Mitchell Wiggins, Nick's team leader in the Portland County Sheriff's Office Search and Rescue team.

Homework now completely forgotten, Nick texted Ruby McClure. "Any chance I can get a ride?" He, Ruby, and a girl named Alexis Frost had all joined SAR at the same time and become friends. Ruby was the only one with a car. Once you were notified, SAR gave you just an hour to get your gear and assemble at the sheriff's office. On a Sunday night, TriMet buses were few and far between.

Ruby texted back a second later. "Sorry. At chamber music concert with parents. Already cutting it close."

Nick jumped to his feet. He needed to change into outdoor gear and grab his SAR backpack and red helmet. And to persuade his mom to let him borrow her car. There was no sense in asking to use his brother's car. If Nick needed to borrow the car to drive to the emergency room or he would die from a collapsed lung or something, Kyle would probably still say no.

Every time he was called out on a SAR mission, he felt closer to his dad, a soldier who had died a hero in Iraq when Nick was only four. His mom was dead set against him ever joining up, but she had agreed to let him be part of SAR.

What he hadn't told her was that SAR was a stepping-stone, a place to acquire skills that would come in handy once he turned eighteen and could enlist. In liberal Portland, there were no high-school-based ROTC programs, but SAR would teach Nick how to track, use knives, give first aid, survive in the wilderness, navigate with a topo map and GPS, and even collect crime scene evidence. He figured that any and all of those would look good to a recruiter.

Ninety minutes later, Nick and twelve other members of SAR's Alpha Team clambered out of the sheriff's white fifteen-passenger van and into the parking lot of a large apartment complex. Jon Partridge, an adult adviser, had driven them to this spot in outer Southeast Portland, past used car lots, strip joints, and fast-food places Nick had never heard of.

In the two months since Nick had joined SAR, he had taken part in five searches for lost hikers and hunters, and two for crime scene evidence. But this was the first time he had been called out for an urban search. When it came to finding people, SAR usually concentrated on the great outdoors. But law enforcement could also mobilize them to search for the vulnerable who might have wandered away: the disabled, the elderly, and children.

Chris Nagle, a sheriff's deputy, was already waiting for them. Aside from Chris and Jon, everyone else standing in the darkened parking lot was a teenager. Most of the other teens were certifieds who had been called out on dozens of searches. Nick, Ruby, and Alexis were allowed to participate in searches, but before they were certified, they needed to complete nine months of training. That included mandatory classes every Wednesday evening and practice outings one weekend a month.

"How could you even remember which apartment was yours?" Alexis asked, turning in a slow circle. The low light made her high cheekbones even more pronounced. Nick tore his gaze away and saw what she meant. They were surrounded by about twenty identical beige buildings, each with three apartments above and three below. All the apartments had dark gray doors, and matching white drapes hung in every window.

"There are myriad minor differences." Ruby's breath clouded the air in front of her fox-like face. "There's the cardinal orientation, the possessions stored on porches, the door decorations . . ."

Nick and Alexis exchanged a look that mingled

exasperation, amusement, and an odd kind of pride. Ruby didn't notice.

Mitchell Wiggins called out, "Huddle up, team!" His long pale hands waved them in. He was already wearing the yellow climbing helmet that marked him as team leader. "Today we will be conducting a hasty search for a seven-year-old girl named Mariana Chavez, who went to play with another child in this complex nearly four hours ago. But the other family wasn't home and she never returned to her own apartment."

Next to Nick, Alexis shivered.

"We'll go door-to-door first," Mitchell continued. "Then we'll clear the grounds. If that fails, we'll check nearby houses, walk roadsides, and clear fields. Remember, we are not only looking for the girl, but we're also looking for any sort of evidence as to her whereabouts."

If Mariana were an adult, this might turn out to be what was known in SAR circles as "a bastard search," when you went looking for someone who had never really been lost at all. But it wasn't nearly as likely that a missing little kid was a false alarm.

"Mariana has shoulder-length black hair," Mitchell continued. "She's wearing black pants, a pink top, a dark blue puffer jacket, and red-and-black rain boots that look like ladybugs. She is in good health and normally not much of a risk taker."

Nick reviewed what they had learned in class about "lost person behavior." Seven was old enough to travel quite a bit farther than even a slightly younger child. But seven was still young enough to be impulsive, or to give in to a desire to explore. Mariana was old enough to have been taught to avoid strangers and yet too young to realize that some strangers meant no harm. So this girl might even hear them calling her name and choose to stay hidden and quiet. Sometimes little kids even fell asleep and slept so deeply they didn't hear searchers calling for them.

Mitchell scanned the circle of volunteers. "Temperatures are forecast to drop below freezing tonight, so if she's out here, it's important we find her."

Nick thought of the two nearby freeways. Somebody could have snatched Mariana and be a hundred miles away by now.

"Does anyone have any questions?" Mitchell asked.

Alexis raised her hand. "What about Mariana's dad? Could he have taken her?"

Chris answered. "Good question, Alexis. We always have to consider if it's a custody situation. But in this case I've spoken to him. He's in Ohio, and he hasn't seen his daughter for two years."

When no one else spoke up, Mitchell said, "Some of these people are probably sleeping. Remember, not everyone is going to react well to being woken up, especially if they hear someone pounding on the door and yelling 'Sheriff's office!' Just say you're with Search and Rescue and keep it at that. Most people will want to help if they know you're looking for a lost child."

Chris cleared his throat. "Of course it's possible that someone who lives in these apartments took Mariana. That's why you need to keep your eyes and ears open as you go door-to-door. But do not intervene. Just observe and report back to Base. And whatever you do, don't go inside, even if they invite you in. If you see anything that makes you the least bit suspicious, don't let on. Just get out of there, come back to Base, and let us know. If someone is holding this little girl against her will, we don't need to give them another hostage."

GLEAMS OF WHITE

MITCHELL QUICKLY BROKE THEM UP INTO teams of two or three. Nick and Ruby were put on the same team as Dimitri, who was a certified. Alexis was teamed up with Ezra and Max, also certifieds.

Each group was given four buildings to clear. Dimitri decided their group would work left to right, top to bottom. Together they went up the stairs. He knocked at the first door with a heavy fist. Nick and Ruby stood behind him. Ruby had a notebook to record anything they learned. With nothing to hold, Nick clasped his hands awkwardly in front of him. He felt like the missionaries his mom was always turning away. Except they only came in pairs. "Search and Rescue," Dimitri called in his heavy accent.

An old woman opened the door. She was pulling an orange cardigan over her maroon flannel pajamas. "Yes?" She looked curiously at their red helmets and SAR backpacks. Her front teeth were missing.

Nick ran his tongue over his teeth.

"Hello, ma'am, we are from Search and Rescue," Dimitri said. "We are looking for a girl. Her name is Mariana Chavez and she is seven years of age. She has dark hair and she is wearing dark clothes and rubber rain boots."

"Oh, I know Mariana!" The old woman clutched her cardigan tighter. "She's missing?"

"I'm afraid so," Nick said as Ruby scribbled something. "But if you do see her or have any information, there will be someone from Search and Rescue in the parking lot you can talk to."

At each new apartment, they met the same lack of success. No one had seen Mariana, although many of them knew the girl or recognized her description. Four of the apartments they tried were dark and no one came to the door.

Lights glowed behind the curtains in the next apartment, but there was no answer to their knock. Did Nick hear movement deep within? He held his breath. What if Mariana were being held captive? Despite what Chris had said, he imagined bursting in, decking the dude with a right hook to the jaw, and then sweeping the little girl up in his arms.

But after a pause, Dimitri just moved on to the next door. When they had canvassed all their assigned apartments, they reported back. Nick tried to tell himself that knowing where Mariana wasn't was as important as knowing where she was.

"Put on your reflective vests and headlamps and take the west side of that road." Mitchell pointed at a dark street bordered by ditches. "Check all open spaces. Backyards if you can see into them. But don't go into any garages or outbuildings."

They crossed the dark street. Ahead of them, the freeway sounded like a river. Nick was beginning to think there was no girl, at least not here, not anymore. Someone had taken her and maybe they would never give her back.

Their flashlights and headlamps probed the darkness as they slowly walked along the empty road next to a vacant scrap of land. The first houses were farther down the road. Nick lifted his flashlight and played it over the dark tangle of weeds, blackberry bushes, and pieces of windblown garbage.

"Mariana!" he yelled, and Dimitri and Ruby joined in. "Mariana! Mariana!"

Nick's flashlight beam picked up a flash of red. His breath catching, he swung it back. But it was just an old McDonald's french fry box.

"Wait!" Dimitri raised his hand. "Are you hearing that?"

Across the street, the blackberry bushes were rustling. Something burst out and ran away. In his headlamp, Nick caught a glimpse of a something small and striped.

"Hello, Mr. Kitten!" Dimitri called out, laughing. He and Ruby turned away.

But farther back, Nick saw a pale flash. "Mariana?" He squinted. Ruby and Dimitri whipped back around. "We're from the sheriff's department. Your mom asked us to look for you."

"I got lost." A girl's voice, thick with tears.

She pushed her way out of the bushes on the far side of the road. The beams of their lights revealed her pale, scratched face and tangled hair. Her eyes were gleams of white, and her rubber boots looked too big for her, bending at the ankle at every step.

"Well, you're not lost now," Ruby called. "We'll take you back to your mom. She's waiting for you."

Suddenly, the girl pushed her way out of the bushes and darted across the street, her arms spread wide.

Just as a pickup barreled around the corner.

GOING IN FOR THE KILL

I T WAS THREE MINUTES PAST ELEVEN WHEN
Lucy Hayes started walking toward the Last Exit. A little
unsteadily because she had pregamed at her apartment.
Sometimes a girl just needed to sing karaoke, especially
Journey's "Don't Stop Believing." But karaoke wasn't nearly
as much fun if you were sober, and even the well drinks at
the Last Exit were five bucks.

Lucy wasn't stupid. She didn't need a DUI, so she was
walking in the freaking cold. Balancing her need to look
cute with the reality of walking fourteen blocks, she had
gone with her black John Fluevog boots with their deco-
rative buttons and hourglass heels. A really stylish girl
might have rocked them in some alternative cyberpunk
version of 1890.

In just a few blocks the wind turned her ears into
chips of ice. She tried pulling up her scarf, but it didn't
help. It even hurt to breathe, the cold air pulling her lungs
inside out.

Finally, Lucy climbed the three steps of what had once been an old house, crossed the front porch (empty now, but crowded in the summer), and pushed open the door with fingers that were numb despite her mittens. Inside it was warm and steamy, and she immediately began to thaw. Up on the tiny stage, a bald guy with long orange sideburns was singing "Billie Jean" while doing a very bad impression of Michael Jackson's moonwalk.

After shoving her mittens into her coat pocket, Lucy took off her purple-and-white-striped scarf. Then she blinked in surprise. Cooper! Cooper was here. He'd said that he thought he was coming down with a cold, that he was going to go to bed early, but here he was, sitting with his shoulders against the wall, laughing at whatever the person facing him had just said.

Before Lucy could call out, wave her hand, hurry over, his eyes began to close and his mouth began to open. And then he was going in for the kill. Leaning in to kiss the girl who had her back to Lucy.

Lucy wanted to rewind time, to put herself back in her apartment, to make it so this was not happening. Because this was not—this couldn't be happening to her.

She didn't remember walking across the room, but suddenly she was right next to them. Cooper and that stupid Jasmine from their econ class, the one with the long waterfall of blond hair, were still locked in a slobbery kiss. When Cooper had told Lucy he didn't like PDA.

Their beers hadn't even been touched. They had probably been too busy kissing.

Lucy's mom had once turned the hose on two strange dogs in the yard. Something like that needed to be done to Cooper and Jasmine.

Leaning past them, she grabbed up the two beers, the glasses slick in her hands, and lifted them high. Their eyes opened just as she upended them. Jasmine squealed and managed to dodge most of hers, but Cooper's plastered his hair to his head.

"What the hell, Cooper!" Lucy shouted. People's heads turned, but she didn't care. Michael Jackson had finished protesting his innocence. The bar was completely silent except for the sound of beer dripping onto the floor.

"Lucy! I can explain." Blinking rapidly, Cooper swiped beer from his eyes. Did he really think there was something he could say that would magically make this all better?

"Explain! I think what's going on is pretty clear!"

Jasmine gave Lucy a sulky look, not even bothering to protest. Her mouth looked swollen. How long had they been kissing tonight? How long had they been kissing in general?

Cooper looked ridiculous. His skull was oddly lumpy. How had Lucy never noticed? Jasmine picked up a napkin and dabbed at her face.

The bartender, an old guy with long, stringy hair, was walking slowly toward them, twisting a once-white bar towel in his hands. "I'm sorry, miss, but you're going to need to leave or I'm going to have to call the cops."

"Don't worry. I'm already going."

She turned on her heel. People were murmuring to

each other. Two or three already had their phones pointed in their direction. Lucy lifted her head. If this got posted someplace on the Internet, she did not want to look like a loser. She stalked out of the bar, not even turning when she heard footsteps hurrying behind her.

STILL AS DEATH

WHAT HAPPENED AFTER MARIANA CALLED out took only a few seconds, but to Ruby, it seemed to last forever.

The girl. Running toward them. Her eyes wide.

Lights rounding the corner. Coming up fast. Too fast. A pickup. Big and black.

Mariana stretched out her arms as if she wanted someone to catch her. Snatch her up and hold her close.

Instead it was the pickup that caught her. Caught her midstride. One moment Mariana was running toward them, and the next she disappeared.

Ruby didn't see the impact, but she heard it. A sickening, meaty thump.

The pickup stopped just past where Mariana had been, so hard it rocked back. Smoke from burning rubber hung in the air.

Mariana was gone, but one of her boots remained in the street. Somehow still standing upright. One red-and-black boot, rocking gently. But where was Mariana?

As the three of them ran around the pickup, toward the place where they had last seen the girl, Dimitri fumbled the radio from the rat pack. "Team Three to Base! Team Three to Base!"

Nick stopped short, and Ruby almost ran into him. He was staring down at the bramble-lined ditch. The girl lay on her side. She was as still as death. One arm flung to the side, the other over her head. One pant-clad leg ended in a white sock. The other ended in a black-and-red boot.

Above the boot was more black and red—and white. The black was her torn pants. The red was her mangled thigh. And the white was a broken bone.

Next to Ruby, Nick suddenly clapped his hand to his mouth, then bent over and threw up on the road.

Ruby pushed past him, already pulling on purple vinyl gloves from the first aid kit in her pack.

Dimitri's radio crackled. "Go ahead, Team Three."

Behind her, someone flung open the truck's door. Hip-hop music spilled out. A young man dressed in jeans and a blue down coat ran around the pickup and stopped short. He was screaming, "Oh my God! Oh my God!"

Ignoring him, Ruby slid down into the ditch.

"We are needing an ambulance right away," Dimitri said in a high-pitched voice. "We found the subject, but she has just been hit by a pickup."

Nick wiped the vomit from his mouth and then lurched toward the girl.

"Talk to me!" Ruby commanded.

The girl didn't move. Was she dead?

With her knuckles she rubbed the girl's sternum. It was

painful but not harmful, designed to provoke a reaction. Only she didn't see one.

She closed her attention to the blood, to the bone, to the guy's denials, to Nick's frightened face, and focused only on the girl's face. She rubbed again, harder.

And was rewarded with the faintest of groans.

"Copy Team Three." Mitchell's voice sharpened. "What's her condition?"

Ruby turned to him. "She's responsive to pain." That meant she was breathing and her heart was beating.

"Oh my God! Did I kill her?" The driver's voice broke. "I killed her!"

Dimitri's words were meant for both Mitchell and the pickup driver. "She is still alive, but her leg is broken open. Perhaps greater injuries. We need an ambulance right away."

"Copy," Mitchell said. "We already made the call. ETA is about five minutes."

Even though they got plenty of first aid training, SAR wasn't what most people considered a fast-response group. It could be hours before they located their subjects, and according to Jon, at that point their main medical concerns would usually be hypothermia or frostbite, not traumatic injuries. By the time SAR showed up, patients were usually either stable—or dead. This situation was nearly unprecedented. But Ruby's parents were doctors, even if they were just dermatologists; and when she was a kid, she had liked looking at their old medical textbooks the way other kids liked looking at Dr. Seuss.

The young man was pacing back and forth on the side

of the road. "She just ran out! Right in front of me! Where did she come from?"

Nick stumbled down into the ditch. He put his hands on the girl's boot. "We've got to get the bone to go back in." He started to lift her foot, and the girl screamed right in Ruby's ear.

"No!" Ruby and Dimitri yelled at the same time.

Nick dropped it. She screamed again, but not as loud.

"The bone could be corking the wound," Ruby said rapidly. "If you try to push it back in, she could bleed out— and you could do even more damage." Should she be saying all this in front of the girl, now that she seemed to be conscious?

"Nick, please hold the C-spine." Dimitri meant the cervical spine. He clambered down next to them. "Ruby, get a bandage from your pack. We need to stop this bleeding. Do not press on the place of the fracture, but above."

"I know," Ruby interrupted him, already ripping open a sterile bandage. "I'll try to find the femoral artery." The femoral ran down the inside front of the leg. She was careful not to touch the wound. Even breathing on it could cause infection. She pressed above the tear in the girl's pants. Under her touch, Mariana began to squirm. Nick was on his belly, propped on his elbows and cradling her head with his palms, but he would be no match if the girl kept moving.

"Mariana," she said, leaning closer. "It will be okay, but you need to stay absolutely still." If the bone fragments got moved around, they could cut her. "So stay still, okay? Do you hear me?"

The girl's eyes were still closed. In the light of Ruby's

headlamp, her lips had a bluish tinge. But then she made the slightest of nods.

"I am checking for the other life threats." Dimitri ran his hands lightly over the girl's head, neck, and then her arms and other leg. She flinched a little at his touch, but Ruby kept murmuring to her that it was okay. And then Dimitri nodded and Ruby knew it really might be, except for the broken bone.

Nick was still holding the C-spine. His face was nearly as white and clammy as the little girl's.

It seemed to take forever, but it was only a few more minutes before two EMTs were sliding down into the ditch to join them. While one wrapped her in a cervical collar, Nick took hold of the girl's hand, murmuring everything would be all right. He only relinquished it when the other paramedic clipped a plastic oximeter to the girl's finger.

"The patient is seven-year-old Mariana Chavez," Ruby told the EMTs as they worked. "Her pulse is 120 and thready. She has a compound fracture of the right femur, but no other observed injuries. We've been holding her C-spine since about thirty seconds after the accident."

Her words were met by nods and a few puzzled looks.

But Ruby was used to that.

EMPTY HANDS

"WAIT! LUCY! WAIT!"

Ignoring Cooper's shouts, Lucy somehow managed to make it down the three steps of the Last Exit's porch. It was hard to focus through her tears.

Just as she reached the sidewalk, he grabbed her arm and pulled her around. People from the bar had spilled out onto the porch and were watching them. Including Jasmine, who was dabbing at her coat with a handful of paper napkins.

"Just talk to me, Lucy!" Cooper's lips were pulled back. For a moment, she wondered if she should be afraid.

"You okay, miss?" a man's voice called out. Cooper threw a glance over his shoulder and then let go.

"I'm okay. Thank you!" she said, eager for everyone to leave them alone.

Looking as embarrassed by the whole scene as Lucy was, a young guy hurried down the steps and past them.

She turned back to Cooper and lowered her voice.

"Why should I talk to you?" She couldn't stand the thought that her biggest humiliation was being witnessed by a dozen strangers. A dozen strangers and Jasmine, which made it even worse. She felt coldly sober now, not the least bit fuzzy. Everything felt sharp but also far away. "There's nothing to say. You're supposed to be *my* boyfriend. Instead you're in some bar kissing *her*." She wasn't going to say Jasmine's name.

"Look, it was nothing. It was, like, an accident." Cooper's beer-soaked head steamed in the cold, little tendrils of fog drifting up in the glow of the streetlamp.

"An accident!" Lucy hissed. "Don't give me that. It didn't even look like your guys' first kiss."

"It's because you won't move in with me." Cooper's voice was low and urgent.

"That doesn't make any sense."

"I just wanted to make you jealous."

She found the flaw in his argument. "And just how was that supposed to work if I never found out?"

"Everyone who comes here is a big gossip. You would have heard."

"That's ridiculous," Lucy said, wondering if his version of the event could possibly be true. "I'm going home now."

Cooper put his hand on her wrist and leaned close. Despite herself, Lucy still felt a flash of desire.

"Let me come with you."

"No!"

Heels clacked down the stairs as Jasmine joined them. "Cooper's the one who brought *me* here," she told Lucy.

"This wasn't my idea. It was his. He's been asking to go out with me for weeks."

"That's not true!" Cooper protested.

Lucy didn't wait to hear any more. She turned on her heel and set off at a determined pace, her head held high. But as she walked, her courage and strength began to leak away. The cold crawled up her sleeves and wrapped around her neck like a muffler. She must have left her scarf at the bar. Along with everything else. Her happiness. Her so-called boyfriend. Her blissful ignorance. She was crying in earnest now.

Her head was a balloon, and her feet didn't belong to her. It was hard to walk when you couldn't see through your tears. As she crossed the street, an old pickup had to stop short, but she barely saw it. A minute later, Lucy's foot slipped on a skim of ice that had glazed a puddle.

"Are you okay?"

She started and turned. A guy. She hadn't even heard him pull up across the street. He had just gotten out of the pickup that had narrowly missed her.

He lifted his empty hands in the air, palms toward her. "Sorry. I didn't mean to scare you. It's just that I heard you crying. Is everything all right?"

"I'm fine." With a sodden mitten, she swiped at her nose.

"Pardon me for saying so, but you don't look fine."

Lucy opened her mouth to speak, but the words wouldn't come. Instead, she just shook her head.

"Can I call you a cab?"

She shook her head again, tears blinding her eyes.

He leaned into his truck and came up with a roll of

white paper towels. Holding it ahead of him, he crossed the street. "Sorry I don't have a handkerchief. But how about a paper towel?"

The ridiculousness of it made Lucy half smile.

He stepped closer.

AN OPEN WOUND

A LEXIS HURRIED OVER AS NICK AND RUBY climbed out of a police cruiser holding their backpacks. "Are you guys okay?" she asked as the cop pulled away from the apartment's parking lot.

She hadn't seen the accident or the aftermath, but all of them had heard it. Unlike a wilderness rescue, when only Base heard everything, tonight the teams had been close enough to catch each other's transmissions. Close enough to hear the wailing sirens of the ambulance and police cars when things went terribly wrong.

Alexis's team hadn't even made it back to Base before the ambulance had done a scoop and run. The guy who'd hit Mariana had also been taken to the hospital for blood tests to see if he'd been drunk or drugged. But it sounded like it had just been a terrible accident.

At her question, Nick shrugged, but his too-wide eyes, shiny in the glow of the streetlight, gave him away. "It was a little gory, but we handled it. Dimitri stayed behind to talk to the cops."

"At least we didn't have to use the ten-code for a deceased subject," Ruby said. The only clue that she had been affected by events was how fast she was chewing her gum. Deaths were one of the few times SAR didn't transmit in plain English. The families of the missing usually hung out around Base, meaning they were often within earshot of a radio.

From behind Alexis, Mitchell demanded, "How in the heck did you guys let a subject get hit by a vehicle? We're going to have to do a boatload of paperwork to explain it!" Even though he had been team leader for only a few weeks, Mitchell was fully invested in the role. He was an Eagle Scout who wanted to be a cop.

"There wasn't any time to react," Ruby said as she stripped off her purple vinyl gloves.

Mitchell's eyes went from her hands to Nick's bare ones. "Nick, where are *your* gloves? Please tell me you were wearing them on scene."

Nick winced. "Sorry. I forgot."

"Let me see your hands." Mitchell's tone was exasperated as he turned on his headlamp and leaned close. "If you have an open wound, then you just got exposed to a biohazard."

"I didn't get any blood on me." Nick held out his hands. They trembled in the beam of light. He made a show of shivering as if he were cold.

Mitchell pointed to the sleeve of his parka. "What are those wet spots?"

He hesitated. "Vomit. Um, my vomit."

"It *was* pretty gross," Ruby said. "Compound fracture."

Alexis was very glad she hadn't been on scene.

Mitchell blew air out of pursed lips. "That is *so* against protocol. We're going to have to debrief tonight."

Ruby stepped in front of Nick. "His skin appears intact, which means his risk is very low. Especially given that the victim is a seven-year-old girl, which means she's probably not infected with hepatitis or HIV. And it's not like he suffered a percutaneous injury with a large, hollow-bore needle."

Alexis nodded at Ruby's words, even though part of her was thinking: *Who even talks like that?*

An hour later, everyone who had responded to the call-out was seated in a circle at the sheriff's office, listening to Dimitri try to explain what had happened.

"The girl, she hid in bushes." Dimitri was rolling his *R*s and hacking up his *H*s even more than usual.

As he sought the right words, Alexis shifted in the uncomfortable plastic chair. Jon had said this was an informal debrief. Still, a lot of people looked tense, and Jon had begun by saying there would be a chaplain available to talk to them. Search and Rescue was supposed to help people. To find an uninjured subject and then see her get hurt while she was being rescued was unheard of.

Dimitri slowed as he sought the words. "First we saw a cat. Then Nick saw girl and called out. Before we realize what was happening, she ran to us."

Alexis had volunteered for SAR because she was determined to have a better life, a life that didn't include food stamps, thrift store clothes, and Medicaid. To do that, she had to go to college. But her guidance counselor had said that if she wanted to snag a scholarship, being poor wasn't enough, not when her grades were unexceptional Bs. Alexis needed something to make herself stand out. And it wasn't like she was a left-handed bassoon player.

So she had joined SAR and then promptly regretted it. Sure, the outdoors was pretty, but not so pretty when you were freezing and your thrift store boots were rubbing your heels raw. Not so pretty when you were crawling inch by slow inch through a muddy field, looking for evidence the cops thought a bad guy might have discarded. Plus there had turned out to be a lot more math than she had expected.

But when Alexis had helped find a hiker lost in the mountains, her feelings had done a 180. The guy—his name was George—had been on the verge of hypothermia. If SAR hadn't found him, he could have died. When George had hugged Alexis, pressing his wet, cold cheek against hers, she had realized it was all worth it.

Now Dimitri made the fingers of one hand run in midair. "At the same time, the pickup came around corner"— he balled his other hand into a fist and bumped it into the running fingers—"and hit girl. Her leg, it was broken. Nick held C-spine, Ruby stopped bleeding, and I checked the life threats."

Jon held up one hand. "And who was responsible for stopping traffic?"

Dimitri, Nick, and Ruby just looked at one another.

Jon spoke into the silence, his voice surprisingly gentle. "Your first responsibility is your own safety."

Nick kicked the carpet with the toe of his boot. "But it all happened so fast."

"I'm sure it did." Jon leaned forward. "The adrenaline

rush usually makes people forget step one, which is"—he turned to Dimitri—"what?"

"Scene safety." Dimitri looked down at his hands. His fist was still bumping into his two fingers.

"That's right. Our first instinct is to save. That's why we're all here. When you see something go down in front of you, you want to help, so you dive right in. But if we don't take steps to keep ourselves safe, then things could get a lot worse instead of better. We're just lucky we didn't end up with four injured people instead of one." He looked at Ruby. "And what's step two after scene safety?"

Ruby straightened up. "PPE. Personal protective equipment."

"Right." Jon looked around the circle. "We'll be talking about this more on Wednesday, but we need to make sure that gloving up is second nature." Nick's shoulders rose, as if he was waiting to be yelled at.

Instead, Jon said, "This is a learning experience. For all of us. Over the next few days, we'll be looking at what we did right and what we could have done better. What happened today, a subject getting hurt, was very unusual. Thankfully we are hearing from the hospital that the girl should recover fully. Still, we want to make sure everyone is feeling okay. We don't want you freaking out on the drive home when you think about what happened. So if any of you would like to talk to the chaplain, he's out in the lobby. We also have some free resources for therapy visits through the sheriff's office." Jon looked at the back of the room. "And good, it looks like TIP was also able to spare us some folks."

As she turned to look, Alexis would not let herself

hope. But then she saw the familiar dark head. Something bloomed in her chest. Bran was here!

Bran—short for Brandon—Dawson was a teen volunteer for Portland's Trauma Intervention Program. He and Alexis had met a few weeks earlier on a different mission, one where her team had found a body. And later, when her mom's health had taken a turn for the worse, he had been there for her.

Now he and Alexis were—something. They hadn't put a name to it. They didn't go to the same school, so they mostly just texted. In some ways, Alexis preferred texting to real-life conversations. You could be light and funny and just present the side of yourself you wanted someone else to see. You could skip over the depressing or boring parts, and you never had a bad hair day. And if you didn't want to answer a text, you didn't—and then later made up an excuse.

She had even kissed Bran once. In a coffee shop in front of a dozen other patrons. Did that really count as a kiss? Because so far the experience hadn't been repeated.

She grinned at Bran. But Bran didn't grin back. In fact, he barely even looked at her. Her stomach lurched. Had she done something to make him mad?

After Jon dismissed them, Dimitri ended up talking to Bran in a corner of the room. Alexis didn't talk to anyone from TIP. Nick didn't, either, although Alexis guessed he needed it at least as much as Dimitri. Ruby, of course, seemed unfazed.

Alexis loitered in the corner, watching Bran. His mouth was crimped, his face more serious than she had ever seen it. At one point, he put his arm around Dimitri's shoulders.

His straight black hair fell across his eyes, hiding his expression.

Ruby came up to her. "Need a ride home?"

Bran glanced over at them. "I've got it, Ruby."

Alexis flushed as people turned to look, trying to read between the lines. TIP volunteers weren't allowed to give rides to people they counseled. Friends—and girlfriends—were different.

But when Bran was finally done talking to Dimitri, he didn't even look at her. He just took his keys from his pocket, saying, "You ready?"

"Sure." In silence, they walked out into the parking lot toward his small brown Honda. *Was* he angry with her?

"Is something wrong, Bran?"

"No. Of course not."

But Alexis heard the lie in his voice.

CHAPTER 9
NICK
SUNDAY

HOT AND BITTER

ON HIS WAY OUT TO THE PARKING LOT, Nick walked behind Alexis and Bran. What kind of a name was Bran, anyway? It sounded like some boring, healthy cereal. Something that would get stuck between your teeth.

Neither one of them seemed to even notice that Nick was right behind them. Alexis was holding on to Bran's arm, her face turned toward him as if he were the sun.

With her free hand, she reached up and pushed the hair out of Bran's eyes. Suddenly Nick's chest hurt, a pain so fierce and sharp it felt like someone had slipped a knife between his ribs and given it a good twist.

The two of them climbed into Bran's small brown car. And they still hadn't seen him. Nick got into his mom's car and slammed the door.

Alexis was nice to Nick, sure. Alexis was his friend.

But that was all.

Even though he had met Alexis first. Even though they sat together in SAR class every Wednesday night and Alexis saved a place for him if she was there before him. Even though she laughed at his jokes and had admired his drawings.

Even though Nick had once saved her life.

But Bran had four inches and forty pounds on Nick. All of it muscle. Plus he was a senior, which meant he was two years older than Nick. And he had his own car, while Nick had a car only if he could wheedle his mom into letting him borrow hers.

And tonight hadn't helped advance his case, Nick thought sourly as he took the exit for the freeway. Not when Mitchell had forced him to admit in front of Alexis that he had thrown up.

Yakking like that had just come out of nowhere. One moment Nick had been looking at Mariana's leg—*oh my God was that white thing really a bone?*—and the next his mouth had flooded with saliva. A second later a column of vomit, hot and bitter, had risen up his throat and pushed past the hand he had tried to hold it back with. It had taken all that he had not to fall to his knees.

After the paramedics had taken over and he had let go of her hand, Nick had realized that his own hand was still wet with either sweat or maybe vomit. Hopefully it had just been sweat. Dimitri had tried to make him feel better. "You did good, Nick. Immediately, you protected her spine. And do not feel bad for the vomiting. It is hard when it is all fresh like that."

Now Nick was stuck behind an old beater pickup doing about thirty-five. What was the guy even doing on the freeway? The next lane over was full of trucks, so he couldn't pass. "Come on," he muttered, gripping the steering wheel so tightly it cut into his palms.

Nick's dad must have sucked it up when he was in Iraq. You could bet that he hadn't been puking on the front lines. You couldn't be a soldier if the sight of a little blood turned your stomach inside out.

His mom never even talked about his dad, who had been dead for a dozen years. But Nick had seen the medal, snug in its case, in her dresser drawer. A Bronze Star on a red, white, and blue ribbon. He had looked it up on Wikipedia. "Rewarded for bravery, acts of merit, or meritorious service."

But his mom never talked about the medal or the man. His dad had fallen in combat—that was all Nick had been able to piece together from cryptic scraps of overheard conversation. Sacrificed himself to save others.

Nick had been four when his dad died. Sometimes he wondered if his few memories, now worn paper thin, were even his. Maybe he had imagined them or seen them in a movie. He thought he remembered a deep, booming voice; big hands lifting him into the air; a scratchy cheek against his own.

All his mom ever said was, "The army destroyed your father. You'll join up over my dead body."

When it was the only thing Nick wanted.

In the army, he was sure he would feel like he belonged. He had this weird pale Afro. He was too light-skinned to be black, too dark-skinned to be white. Nick had grown up in a white world, but he didn't really fit there. That world didn't really want him. If he went into a store with a white friend, his friend would be left alone, while Nick would be followed.

But in the army, Nick was sure he would fit in. All the army asked was that you be fit and strong and fast. And brave. And until tonight, Nick had thought he was well on his way to getting there.

Finally, he spotted a chance to pass the pickup, and he took it, even though his mom's car shuddered, even though his exit was just ahead.

What would his dad think now if he could see Nick? Vomiting and nearly passing out when he should have been helping a little girl? Yeah, sure, he had eventually pulled it together, but what if it kept happening every time he saw blood? If he joined up, could he even make it through basic training, let alone an actual firefight?

Nick was a failure. As a potential boyfriend and a potential soldier. With an index finger, he punched the button on his mom's radio so that it switched from the golden oldies station to something a lot more angry. Something that fit his mood.

CHAPTER 10

K

SUNDAY

MONSTER

WHAT HAD HE DONE? *WHAT HAD HE DONE?* In the small bathroom, he threw up and kept throwing up until all that came out were strings of yellow bile.

He was a monster.

No. What had happened was a mistake. A mistake he would never make again.

That was what he told himself. Over and over.

FULL OF BLOOD AND SCREAMS

NICK WAS TOO KEYED UP TO SLEEP. Images kept flickering through his brain. Alexis hanging on to Bran. Mariana's mangled leg. Alexis brushing the hair out of Bran's eyes. The weight of Mariana's skull in Nick's hands. Interspersed with pictures of other things, darker things.

What kind of dreams would he have, full of blood and screams? He most definitely did not want to go to bed right away.

With luck, Kyle would be up, he thought as he put his key in the door. Or at least he would get up once he heard Nick. He let the front door thump closed. Their mom slept so hard that nothing could wake her, but Kyle was a light sleeper.

Nick needed to let off steam. To get out some of the energy still humming in his veins. He and Kyle could play a little *Call of Duty*. It would be way more fun without Mom hovering in the background, looking appalled. She claimed *COD* was too violent.

Violent it might be, but Nick already knew that a two-dimensional image and some shouts and sound effects weren't much like real life. It sure didn't include the coppery scent of blood, or the way a girl's face felt under your fingertips as she walked the frayed rope between life and death. The very falsity of a video game was comforting. When the game was over, you just put down your controller and went back to your real life.

And while they were shooting and stabbing and running, Nick would tell Kyle some of the truth about what had happened tonight. Not all of it, of course. He didn't want to see Kyle's disgust. But he would tell him how he had helped save Mariana's life.

Sure, Ruby had been the one trying to stop the bleeding, but in some ways stabilizing Mariana's cervical spine—or C-spine—had been even more important. Since the pickup had hit her hard enough to knock her out of one of her boots, it might have also broken something inside the slender column of her neck. And if that had happened and Mariana moved, then those shattered bits of bone could have sliced into her spinal cord. A seven-year-old permanently in a wheelchair—maybe even needing a machine to breathe for her—was even worse than a seven-year-old with a mangled leg.

Until the paramedics arrived with a cervical collar, Nick's job had been to be the human version. He had laid on the damp ground behind her, propped on his elbows, his thumbs above her ears, his fingers cradling the bones at the back of her skull. Just as they had been taught, he didn't try to move Mariana's head, or carry the entire weight of it. He simply held it in place.

Under his thumbs, Mariana's face had been cool and clammy, which meant she was already going into shock. He and Ruby had told her over and over not to turn her head, that everything was okay, that she needed to lie still, that help was on the way.

When the paramedics showed up, it took them only a few seconds to wrap a real cervical collar around her neck, bandage her leg, and thank all of them for what they had done. He had held her hand until the last possible moment, been rewarded by a squeeze when he told her he had to let go. Then they had put her on a backboard and loaded her into the ambulance.

Nick's stomach had calmed down since it first rebelled. Now he rummaged through the refrigerator, letting the jars and bottles clank together, listening for the sound of Kyle's bedroom door opening.

Silence.

He allowed the fridge door to thump into place. No answering sound of Kyle's bedroom door opening. After pulling a box of cereal off the shelf, he let the cupboard door slam closed.

Nothing.

Finally, he went to his brother's bedroom door. Nick listened, holding his breath, then turned the handle and nudged it open.

Kyle's bed was empty.

BEADED WITH BLOOD

HE SHOWERED UNTIL ALL TRACES OF HER were gone. Scrubbed with a loofah until every inch of his body was pink and tender. Every bit of skin was new now. Beaded with blood here and there.

Blood. He couldn't think about blood, or he would get sick again.

He couldn't believe he had done it.

Done that thing.

But he hadn't meant to.

Had he?

And now he might go to jail for the rest of his life.

For a one-minute mistake.

For a mistake he would take back if he only could.

ONCE YOU KNEW THE TRICK

THAD WESTMORELAND RODE WITH HIS head down. Bad enough that it was icy this morning. There was also a wind that seemed to be funneling right down the collar of his jacket.

Riding a bike to work had been great when it had been warm. Now, even dressed in a waterproof jacket and pants, there were many days it was a wet slog. Today it was simply bone-chillingly cold. But on minimum wage and working part-time, who could afford a car? The irony was that his job was at the car wash, where he spent all day telling people, "Neutral, no brakes, hands off the wheel."

This time of year, most Portlanders didn't bother to wash their cars. Not when the rain did most of the work for them and there wasn't any sun to show the remaining dirt. When the weather turned in late October, Thad's hours had been cut back, but at least his job hadn't completely disappeared.

He pedaled on, already sweating through the white

polyester shirt and the clip-on tie they all had to wear, as if they worked in an office.

If only he'd wrapped a scarf around his neck this morning. He lifted one hand from the handlebars to see if he could pull the zipper on his jacket any higher. As he did, his messenger bag slid around his torso. When he tried to push it back, he started to lose his balance. Just before he tipped over, he managed to get his foot down.

As he readjusted his bag, Thad looked out across the empty patch of land. Years ago, he thought, there had been an apartment building here. Now there was nothing. Part of it was level and part of it sloped. During the wet part of the year, which was about eight months, there was a tiny creek down there, winding between blackberry bushes.

But today the space held something more than just iced-over water and weeds. He squinted. It was a boot. A woman's black boot.

It was more than just a boot, he realized. There was a *leg* in that boot. He traced it back. It was like one of those puzzles, the ones with the captions that asked, "What do you see?" When he was a kid, Thad had always liked those puzzles. Where things suddenly fell into place if you stepped back or let your eyes go blurry or even looked away. Once you knew the trick, it was easy to see the truth.

And the truth was that he was pretty sure there was a body lying down there.

He got off his bike, leaned it against a telephone pole, and ventured closer. Ice-rimmed weeds brushed against his legs, and he was glad of his waterproof pants. As he got closer, his footsteps slowed down. Finally, he was close enough to peer over a patch of blackberry canes that hid the top part of the body from view.

Arms and a face. A young woman's face.

So, so white that Thad let out the breath he had been subconsciously holding. It couldn't be a person. It had to be a mannequin. Human beings did not come in that weird waxy shade, a skim-milk white verging on blue. Besides, bodies didn't just appear in vacant lots in Southwest Portland.

Then he realized that mannequins didn't, either.

And now he saw where all the color had gone. The ground under her held a dark red pool.

"Lady!" he said. For some reason he found himself whispering, as if she were asleep. "Lady!"

She lay on her back, a small woman, no more than five two or three. She looked about his age, somewhere between twenty and twenty-five. A fan of wet, dark hair surrounded her face. One corner of her forehead looked abraded. Her arms were outstretched. A yellow purse was looped around her left elbow. Her lips were purple, and not from lipstick. Her eyes were half open.

"Lady!" Thad made his whisper louder.

The eyes didn't blink. She didn't move at all.

He had to get closer. Had to see if she was alive. He climbed down the slope, but after his first step, he started to slide. His Converses found no purchase on the frosted weeds. He pinwheeled his arms as he began to lose his balance.

Thad would later tell the police he wasn't sure why he had decided to check out the body before calling 9-1-1. Was it because he thought she might still be alive? Was it because he still wasn't sure she was really a person?

Whatever the reason, at 6:51 that morning, Thad Westmoreland landed with a thud a foot away from a body. He levered himself up onto his elbows, his face just inches from a dead girl's.

And then she gasped.

SOMETHING REALLY BAD

Nick woke to the sound of sirens screaming up his street. He sat up. His mouth tasted sour. Like something had died on his tongue.

Last night he had eaten two bowls of Life cereal and a sleeve of Ritz crackers chased with a glass of orange juice while he waited in vain for Kyle to show up.

The weird thing was that even though Kyle hadn't been home, when Nick had pushed aside the curtain to check, his old white GTI had been parked on the street. So where had he been? Kyle didn't even have a girlfriend at the moment, at least not one that Nick knew about.

Now Nick shambled down the hall. Kyle must have come home, because here he was, in body if not quite in spirit, slumped over a bowl of Wheaties slowly turning into brown mush. His chin was propped up with one hand, while with the other he scrolled through texts with his thumb. He glanced up at Nick, but it was hard to read his expression because his hand covered his mouth. His eyes were at half-mast. Even when he wasn't out late at night doing who knows what, Kyle was always tired. During the day, he sorted packages at UPS. At night, he was inching his way to an associate degree at Portland Community College, one or two evening classes at a time.

"I didn't even hear you come in last night, Nick," his mom said.

He and Kyle exchanged a look. What was his brother thinking? He didn't look guilty or proud or anything. Still, there was something off about him this morning. Kyle had lighter skin than Nick, but today it seemed a weird washed-out tint, nearly verging on green.

Carrying her coffee mug, his mom walked over to Nick and touched his cheek. "What happened to you? It looks like you got into a catfight—and lost."

Nick touched his fingertips to the same spot and found three shallow furrows, dotted and dashed with tiny scabs. He didn't even remember getting them, but he had been so focused on getting to Mariana.

How much of her story should he tell? Better to stick to the bare minimum. "We found a little girl who had gotten lost chasing after a kitten. She was in some blackberry bushes."

"So she's okay?"

"Yeah. Basically." Another siren whooped up their street.

His mom's head turned as she followed the sound. "That's got to be the third or fourth one I've heard in thirty

49

minutes. Something really bad must have happened—and close by."

Kyle's hand suddenly tightened against his mouth. He leapt to his feet, pushed past Nick, and then bolted out of the room. Down the hall, the bathroom door slammed, but it didn't do much to conceal the sound of his retching. Nick hadn't been that hungry, and now the idea of food didn't seem appealing at all.

"It sounds like Kyle has the flu." His mom's mouth twisted as Kyle made another terrible noise. "Half the people in my checkout lane have been sick. You look at the belt and it's loaded up with cough drops and NyQuil and you just wonder what your chances are." She was a cashier at Fred Meyer, a regional supermarket chain. "I keep using hand sanitizer, but it doesn't help if people are coughing or sneezing right in your face."

When he got really upset or anxious, Kyle sometimes threw up. Same as Nick. Nick still felt a little queasy when he thought about what had happened last night.

So was something bothering Kyle or was it just a stomach bug? Whatever the truth was, Nick felt better about yakking when he first looked at Mariana's leg. Throwing up was a trait he shared with his brother. Didn't that mean it had to be genetic? His mom had a cast-iron stomach. You could bring her a dead frog, show her a nasty cut, or even throw up on her shoes and she would just carry on. So if Nick's and Kyle's sensitive stomachs hadn't come from her, they must have inherited them from their dad. Which meant it must not have stopped him from serving in the army.

"You'd better hurry up and eat." The coffeemaker hissed when she pulled the pot free while more fresh coffee was still trickling in. She dumped the few ounces into her mug and slid the pot back. She never ate breakfast but always insisted that they did.

Nick hadn't even sat down at the table, where Kyle's cereal was entering the last stages of Wheaties soup. "I think I'll grab something to eat later."

"Don't tell me you're getting sick, too!" She tried to put the back of her hand on his forehead, but he ducked away.

"No. But listening to Kyle has kinda put me off eating for a while."

"Okay." She went to her purse and dug out a five-dollar bill. "In case you want to buy something at school." She held it out to him.

He shoved it into his jeans pocket. "Thanks."

From his room, his phone started chirping. When he checked, there was a text from Mitchell.

Evidence search in SW Portland. Meet @ 0900.

As Nick read, he heard another siren. His room faced the backyard, so he couldn't see anything. Carrying his phone, he walked down the hall and out the front door.

Barefoot, he picked his way across the lawn, shivering in his T-shirt. The blades of grass were edged with the white sparkle of frozen dew. In his wake, he left clear green footprints. He reached the curb and kept walking until he got to the corner. He looked up the street. About six blocks away, something was clearly up. He squinted. A fire truck and maybe a half-dozen cop cars.

Nick texted back. Is that anywhere near Greenleaf?

It's ON Greenleaf. How did you know?

Nick's heart started thumping like a phone book in a dryer. Because I'm right down the street.

EVERYDAY CARRY

NICK WALKED BACK THROUGH HIS YARD, now with his phone pressed against his ear. Normally he would have just kept texting, but he was calling Mitchell instead. Cautious Mitchell might *say* something that he would never text.

When Nick opened the door, Kyle was in the living room, watching some sports recap on TV. "What's going—" his brother started, but Nick raised his hand, telling him it would have to wait. He walked straight back to his room.

"'This is Nick," he said when Mitchell finally answered. "I live right off Greenleaf. What's going on?"

"A female crime victim was discovered in a vacant lot on Greenleaf this morning."

Nick knew that lot. When he was a little kid, it had held a small apartment complex. Then some idiot shooting off illegal bottle rockets on the Fourth of July had sent one through a window instead of up into the sky. He had vague memories of being part of a crowd watching the orange flames leap into the darkness.

The tenants had made it out safely, but the building itself had been a total loss. The remains had been bull-dozed but the place was never rebuilt. His mom had said it had something to do with the trickle of water that ran through the lot during the rainy months. Now the space was covered with blackberry bushes and weeds.

"So she's dead?" Nick lifted his SAR backpack from the floor of his closet and laid it on the bed. He stepped out of his jeans as he pulled a set of long underwear from his dresser. You couldn't wear jeans on a callout. Once they got wet, the cotton would just suck the heat right out of you. SAR protocol called for wearing three layers, top and bottom. You started with a base layer of long underwear, added fleece for insulation, and topped it with something waterproof.

"I heard she was alive at the scene, but just barely. I don't know what's happened since then. She was stabbed, probably sometime last night."

Nick couldn't believe it. A murder or an attempted murder, right in his neighborhood?

The hour he had to get dressed, get his gear, and get to the sheriff's office was ticking away. It was ridiculous to have to go through all of that when today's crime scene was just up the street.

"How about if I just meet you guys there?" He pulled on one layer, then another. A murder! And what? Six, seven blocks from his house? Last night he had driven right down Greenleaf, he thought as he hopped on one foot and then the other, pulling up his socks. Maybe around the same time it had happened.

"That's not established procedure," Mitchell said

slowly. Before he went to the bathroom, he probably checked a book of rules to make sure it was okay and to see how many squares of toilet paper he was allowed to use.

Nick forced himself to speak slowly. "Look. It doesn't make sense for me to have to walk to the bus stop, then wait there until the next bus comes, and then get on and wait some more while it makes two dozen stops, and *then* walk the rest of the way to the sheriff's office—and to try to do it all in an hour—when all I would be doing is climbing into a van and coming right back to where I already *am* now." He pushed his feet into his boots.

"I don't know . . ." Mitchell's voice trailed off, and Nick knew he had won. "You're going to have to walk. We can't have a bunch of random civilian cars cluttering up the scene and being a distraction."

Just how lazy did Mitchell think he was? "Don't worry, dude. It's only, like, six blocks away. Of course I'm gonna walk it." Nick didn't bother mentioning that he didn't have a car and that there was no chance he could borrow one today.

"Then it's okay, I guess. See you there."

Before picking up his backpack, Nick opened his dresser drawer, pushed aside the top layer of socks, and looked at the two knives nestled in the back. Every certified member of SAR seemed to carry a knife, sometimes more than one. Knives could cut clothing to gain access to a wound, snip laces to get someone's boot off, even slice seat belts to free someone trapped in a totaled car. Nick had never actually done any of those things yet, or even seen them done, but when Jon had talked about them in one of the Wednesday night classes, he had pictured them plainly. Even doodled a few of the possibilities. And he had saved up and bought his first knife as soon as he could.

Now Nick slipped the Kershaw Blackout into his right pocket. The Kershaw was his everyday carry, or EDC, and he did carry it everywhere. Even at school, which had the kind of sissy policies that would probably get you in trouble for cutting an L-shaped piece of paper and then pointing it at someone. He just kept it buried deep in one of his front pockets. Luckily, Wilson did not have metal detectors.

Nick had saved for several weeks to buy the Kershaw, which was made by a local company. The best part about it was that it was "spring assisted," making it basically similar to a switchblade. Once you pressed the button on the side, it unfolded so fast you couldn't even see it move. Unlike a switchblade, Jon had assured them that spring-assisted knives were legal in Oregon.

Nick left the first knife he had gotten in the drawer. It was a fixed-blade knife, marketed as a "combat knife." He had ordered it off the Internet the day he joined SAR. On their first mission, Nick had worn it in a sheath threaded through his belt, with the handle showing. Five minutes later Jon had taken him aside and told him he had to stow it in his pack.

"Sure, when we're doing survival scenarios, and building shelters and fires and such, a fixed-blade knife might come in handy," Jon had said. "But we don't want people wearing them out in the open all the time. It can make us look a bit military and intimidating." He had actually said these things like they were bad. "It's also about safety. If you trip and fall while you're wearing a fixed-blade knife, it's possible it could punch right through the sheath, and maybe even into you. So you're going to have to stash it." After that, Nick had bought the Kershaw and put the combat knife in his sock drawer.

Once Nick started carrying a knife, it turned out you could use it surprisingly often. No need to look for scissors when you had to cut something. And he *had* used it in SAR for less dramatic things, like cutting parachute cord for shelters, cutting the string that marked out grid searches, and breaking down wood to build a fire.

Dressed in his outdoor gear, Nick hoisted his helmet and backpack. He felt kind of silly carrying his full SAR backpack to a vacant lot in the middle of a city, but Jon said you never knew when you might be called to deploy straight to a trailhead to search for a missing person. Saving a life trumped finding crime scene evidence.

When he came out of his room, Kyle was waiting for him. "So what's happening? What were all the sirens about?"

"I guess some girl got stabbed up the street." Nick put on a nonchalant expression. "SAR got tapped to do the evidence search." Students were allowed to take part in searches during the day, as long as they maintained a certain grade level.

Kyle's eyes actually widened.

For once, his brother was impressed.

DROVE RIGHT BY

WITH EVERY STEP NICK GOT CLOSER TO the scene, his heart rate sped up. He counted eight—no, nine—cop cars. A fire truck sat at the curb. Its ladder had been extended high over the site. At the top, a man was taking pictures, getting an aerial view. Yellow crime scene tape had been looped around trees and signposts and even the antenna of a parked car. A lady cop was stringing up more tape, creating a second perimeter that was probably thirty feet farther out than the first.

Nick wasn't the only one drawn by the sirens. People clutching mugs of coffee stood in their driveways, gawking. Some gathered in groups of two or three, pointing and talking in low but excited voices. And some were already bellying up against the new crime scene tape.

A block from the site, he buckled on his red climbing helmet. The helmet was part of SAR protocol, even if they were in no danger of being bonked by falling rocks. He felt ridiculous wearing it. Bad enough to wear the helmet when you were surrounded by people wearing helmets.

Far worse if it was just you. What if someone thought he was some mentally disabled kid, the kind who had seizures?

But since his orange SAR shirt was covered by his coat, he needed to wear the helmet if he wanted to get on the other side of those two lines of yellow tape. It was like a secret signal that he belonged.

When Nick came up to the crime scene tape, he picked a spot that wasn't yet lined with people. He felt their eyes on him. He wiped all expression from his face as he cut between an old man and a woman wearing a coat over pajamas. He was a professional.

But to get under the tape he had to bend so low the weight of his pack made him stagger. He almost fell. And when he straightened up, a uniformed cop holding a clipboard was glaring at him.

"Just what do you think you're doing? Don't you see that tape?"

Nick was still fumbling for an answer when a man's voice broke in.

"Hey, it's okay, Rob." It was Detective Harriman. They had met when Nick, Alexis, and Ruby had found a girl's body in Forest Park when they were looking for a missing autistic man. "He's with Search and Rescue. They're gonna do our evidence search today." He looked past Nick, and his wrinkles got even deeper as he squinted. "Where's the rest of your crew?"

"They're still coming. I got permission to walk over since I only live about six blocks away." Nick took in the scene. Two cops were talking to the people lined up along the tape. Two more were taking photos of a narrow trail

59

of flattened weeds. And, with a little thrill, he saw a fifth cop using gloved hands to put what looked like a brick into a brown paper bag preprinted with the word *Evidence*. Most of the cops, like Harriman, wore paper booties, but no one was wearing a full-on white suit as Nick had seen on TV shows. He was kind of disappointed.

"How come they're not wearing bunny suits?" Nick asked.

Harriman rolled his eyes. "Think about it. Nearly one hundred percent of the time, if you've got someone in a Tyvek suit, they're standing right next to someone who is not in Tyvek. Our uniforms don't shed. There's no point in suiting up."

"Then why are you wearing booties?"

"Because I don't want to haul back biohazards on the soles of my shoes."

Biohazards was what they called all the stuff that leaked out of dead people. Nick only now registered that the bottoms of Harriman's booties were stained reddish-brown. He swallowed hard and looked away. "This is so weird. I drove right by here last night."

Harriman stepped closer. "What?"

"We had a callout last night near Gresham. Little girl who disappeared. Turned out she had chased after a kitten and gotten lost."

"Yeah, yeah." Harriman waved his hand impatiently. "But what about here? When did you drive by here? What did you see?"

Nick tried to remember what he had seen. Parts of last night were a blur. What had happened after he left the sheriff's office? He remembered being angry at Alexis and

Bran, feeling left out and lonely. He remembered punching the buttons on his mom's car radio, trying to find some music to match his mood. But the drive? That part he didn't really remember. Something about someone driving too slow?

"It was around eleven. I don't think there was anything out of the ordinary. Otherwise, I would have remembered it."

Harriman took out his phone, clicked a few buttons, and then held it out to Nick. A dark-haired young woman stared back at him with a half smile. She had a heart-shaped face, high cheekbones, and a pointed chin. "Have you seen this woman?"

"Last night?"

"Ever. She lives in some apartments a few blocks from you."

Something about her was familiar. Wasn't it?

JUST LOGICAL

RUBY REGARDED THE TWO ROWS OF yellow crime scene tape, one inside the other. On three sides of the vacant lot, there was only one length of tape, but on the side where the van had let them out, two lengths of tape ran parallel to each other, about thirty feet apart. Why? Part of the space between had been portioned off into a large square that held three adults: a man with a notebook, a woman with a microphone, and another man with a TV camera.

Nick was already here, talking to Detective Harriman. Ruby had felt a pinch of jealousy when he had texted her that he had persuaded Mitch to let him walk to the scene. Shoot, she could have driven here in half the time it had taken her to get to the sheriff's office and then take the van. It could have been her talking to Detective Harriman.

"Put your packs over there." Mitchell lifted the first row of tape for them and pointed at a spot that already held Nick's pack. "Next to the box for the media." Ruby, Alexis, and the eight other teens who had been in the van set down their backpacks. The female reporter, who was wearing a long red quilted coat, pointed at them. "Get some footage of the kids, Frank. It'll be good B-roll."

Mitchell led them to the far side of the square, where Detective Harriman and Nick waited with Jon. "Okay," Detective Harriman said without preamble once they had joined him. "Before seven this morning, a guy was biking to work down this street. He saw a boot near those blackberry bushes behind me. When he went to check it out, he found a girl. She'd been stabbed once in the back. We believe the stabbing occurred near that evidence marker"—he pointed at a plastic placard marked with the number seven— "and then she ran, fell, and was bashed in the back of the head and dragged to the spot where she was found. We've already located the brick we believe was used, but we haven't located the knife."

Ruby listened to him as she watched a crime scene detective measure and photograph the drag marks. The trail of laid-down weeds was skinny, about forty feet long and a little over a foot wide. It started near one blackberry bush and ended near another on ground that sloped steeply to a tiny creek.

"When the passerby found her, she was still alive, although unconscious. 9-1-1 dispatched an ambulance, and an officer rode with her in case she said something." Harriman sighed. "But we got word a little bit ago that she died without ever regaining consciousness."

Ruby knew that if the victim had said anything, it would have been a dying declaration, one of the few times hearsay was allowed in court.

"If the knife was discarded in this lot, we need to find it. That's where you guys come in."

"Why can't we just get a metal detector?" Nick asked.

Ruby rolled her eyes. Nick was standing next to her, but she didn't care if he saw. Sure, he was her friend, but his question was uninformed.

It was Mitchell who answered. "A metal detector would just distract us. A knife is a big enough target that if it's here, we should have no problem spotting it by eye. This lot used to hold an apartment complex, so there're still pipes and gas lines underground, as well as whatever garbage has been dumped or buried here over the years. If we used a metal detector, we'd get hundreds of hits that would end up meaning nothing."

"Besides," Detective Harriman cut in, "it's not just the knife. There could even be another weapon, like a gun, that was used to get her to this point. We're also looking for anything the killer might have left behind in a struggle— a glove, a torn piece of clothing, even a clump of hair. We need you looking for anything and everything that can help us solve this murder, whether it's a cigarette, a discarded beer bottle, a piece of gum, or a footprint."

"That's why we can't take any shortcuts," Mitchell said, looking right at Nick. "I know a lot of you were on that search last night and are tired, but remember that we only get one chance to get this right. There are no do-overs. We can't put the evidence back in place and try again. Anything we don't discover today could be lost or damaged—which means it can't be used to get the person who did this."

Even though the girl was past talking, Ruby knew her

body and her belongings could still speak for her. The autopsy would reveal the cause of her death. The toxicology reports would show whether she had been drugged or drunk, although not whether it had been by her killer or by her own choice. There could be fingerprints on her purse, fingerprints that could not only be matched to the killer, but could also have enough DNA to link them to the person who had left them. The girl's clothes and even her skin might yield more DNA from her killer. Or a fiber or hair might be found on her that had actually started out on the killer.

"Locard's exchange principle," Alexis murmured next to Ruby, startling her. Ruby loved to talk about Locard, but she was used to people not listening. Locard's exchange principle felt beautiful because it was so balanced. So logical.

A hundred years ago a French scientist named Edmond Locard had developed a theory that every criminal inadvertently left something at the scene of the crime, while at the same time taking something back with him. A criminal might leave all sorts of evidence, including fingerprints, footprints, even fragments of skin. And by coming into contact with things at a crime scene, Locard postulated, that criminal also took part of that scene with him when he left, in the form of dirt, hair, or other trace evidence.

In 1912 Frenchwoman Marie Latelle had been found strangled in her parents' home. Her boyfriend, Emile Gourbin, was questioned by police but claimed that at the time of the murder, he had been playing cards with friends. The friends backed up his story.

But Locard went to Emile's jail cell and scraped under his fingernails. Under the microscope, he saw skin cells, but in those days there was no DNA testing to show that they had come from Marie's neck. He also saw a pink dust, which he identified as rice starch, the main ingredient of face powder. There was bismuth, magnesium stearate, zinc oxide, and an iron oxide pigment called Venetian red.

And luckily for Locard, in 1912, makeup was not being mass-produced. Marie's face powder was prepared for her by a druggist in Lyon—using those exact ingredients.

Confronted by this evidence, Gourbin confessed to the murder. He also admitted that he had set the clock in his gaming room ahead and then gotten his friends drunk. Later, not realizing the time was wrong, they had provided him with an alibi.

Locard's exchange principle had worked.

Now Mitchell's radio crackled. After a short conversation, he looked up at them. "Okay, guys, we've got a few more members from Team Delta who were able to come out on the search. We're going to wait for them to get here."

The other team members started talking to each other, but Ruby went straight up to Detective Harriman. "Why are there two perimeters on that one side, not one? There was only one perimeter when we did that evidence search in Forest Park."

He sighed. "Aren't you guys on break?"

Ruby said nothing. Normal people were as uncomfortable with silence as she was with looking people in the eye. And after a while, they gave in to the urge to fill it.

Eventually, the same held true for Harriman. "That's because hardly anyone was going to hike all the way out to *that* crime scene. But this—it's in the middle of the city. We've already got gawkers." He indicated the people lined up along the tape. "That outside perimeter is for the general public. The inside one, that's for the bigwigs and the press. They get to duck under the first crime scene tape. They feel special, like they're getting better access. But really, they're no closer than I would let them get if this crime scene were out in the middle of nowhere and no one wanted to see it. I set off the same initial perimeter. It's just for a case like this, a case where you know there's going to be a lot of demand to be treated special, I set up a second barrier outside the first one."

"So how do you know where to set up the first perimeter?"

"My rule is you want to rope off at least one hundred feet from the farthest item of visible evidence. Since all we have right now is the spot where the girl was found and the brick and I'm hoping to find more, I had them set the crime scene tape 250 feet from there. We don't need anybody destroying evidence by walking on it or picking it up. Some people will tell you this amount of space is too big, but it's way easier to make it smaller than to make it bigger."

"That makes sense." Ruby appreciated the logic of it.

He was staring straight into her eyes. "Why do you ask so many questions, anyway?"

Ruby had to look away. What did Harriman think of her? More than once she had been accused of being shifty or dishonest.

After a pause, she said in a rush, "I want to be a cop. Actually, I want to be a homicide detective. Like you." It was the first time she had ever told anyone.

After a pause he said, "You're observant. So that's good. But you need some better people skills. Maybe try not to be so blunt."

Blunt was what people called it when you said what everyone was already thinking.

"I'm just logical. I'm aware that can cause problems because ordinary conversation doesn't always proceed logically, and I'm working to improve that." Ruby took a deep breath. "Besides, I'm no more blunt than you are."

His laugh sounded like a bark. "You might be right about that, Ruby. You might be right."

BETWEEN MEMORY AND NIGHTMARE

A SCREAMING SIREN HAD TORN HIM FROM his dreams. Or not dreams, exactly. He had been someplace halfway between memory and nightmare. In a place where she had made that sound, a desperate intake of breath. In a place where his knife flashed silver in the moonlight. In a place where blood steamed in the icy air.

He lay panting on his pillow. It was real. *It was real.* What would his mother think if she knew?

Another siren. And another and another.

Before he even got out of bed, he called in sick to work. It wasn't really a lie. He was sick, especially when he thought about what might happen to him.

And then he waited. Waited until there were dozens of people lined up along the crime scene tape. All of them there because of what he had done, but none of them knew.

In his ball cap, he blended in. Just one more gawker. One more lookie-lou. He moved among them, but they did not know him. They had no idea. No idea of what he was capable of.

Until last night, even *he* hadn't known.

He took his hands from his pockets and looked down at them. They weren't shaking at all. Last night his hands had done what had to be done. Had done it before his brain or his heart could give a different order.

He was just lucky that he had been wearing gloves. Afterward, when he got home, he had thrown them into the woodstove, ignoring the stench, poking at them until they were nothing but ash. Just like his life.

His mind kept returning to what had happened, playing it over and over.

One minute he had been offering her some comfort. The next she had given him a tremulous smile as she reached for the paper towel to wipe her face, her cheeks streaked with mascara.

Then he stepped forward and tried to put his arm around her. He hadn't meant anything by it, just one human being comforting another in crisis. But her face changed. Her eyes narrowed, her lips pulled back. And then she had turned and run. Run in those ridiculous boots of hers.

He imagined what was going to happen. She was going to call the police. And she was going to claim that he had attacked her. When that was not what had happened at all.

He ran after her. In less than a dozen strides, he caught up with her and grabbed her wrist. She snapped back to him like the final roller skater in a game of crack the whip. They stared at each other, breathing hard. Only each of her breaths ended with a whimper.

"Calm down and listen to me." His voice was an urgent hiss. "Listen to me!"

But she wouldn't listen. She wouldn't even be still. She twisted and turned in his grasp, looking at him like he was a monster. Then she opened her mouth and sucked in her breath, getting ready to scream.

How could he persuade her to be quiet? And then he remembered the knife, the knife that was as much a part of him as one of his fingers. He slipped it free, the blade glinting in the streetlight. He just meant to scare her into silence.

Looking back, he was nearly certain of this.

Her eyes were so wide they showed the whites on either side. She twisted her arm and suddenly she was free and making a run for it. He grabbed her shoulder and yanked her back.

So hard that he pulled her into him. Into him—and into the knife.

He didn't have time to think about what had just happened before she rabbited off. The knife still in her back. He chased her. In the dark. Through the vacant lot. And then her feet tangled and she fell.

The brick was in his fist before he was even aware he had picked it up from the ground. And then it came down on the back of her head.

After it was over, he let the brick fall and braced his hands on his knees, gasping. He hadn't meant for any of this to happen. He wasn't even sure how it *had* happened.

His gorge heaved, but he clamped his lips closed. There must be some way he could fix this.

Some way that didn't end with him strapped to a gurney and a prison doctor injecting him with poison.

Nothing he could do would bring this girl back.

A car went down the street. He froze. Had they seen him? Or—more important—had they seen her? Seen him with her?

He had to get out of here. Right now. But if he left her here, she was in clear sight of the street. He grabbed her under the arms and started to drag her. Then he saw the knife. He was wearing gloves—thank goodness for that—but the knife might still be traced back to him. He had to step on her back to wrench it free. Not knowing what else to do with it, he put it back in its sheath.

He started pulling at her again. He lifted heavy boxes all day, but this took every ounce of his strength. When he got to the part where the ground began to slope, he let go. She tumbled, boneless, until she was half hidden by a blackberry bush. She might not even be found for a while.

Shaking, trembling, he had left. Burned his gloves, soaked his knife in bleach, scrubbed his skin raw in the shower. He didn't even know her name. There was nothing to connect them.

Was there?

HOW A RABBIT FELT

AFTER THE PEOPLE FROM TEAM DELTA arrived, Mitchell clapped his hands. "Okay, people, line up and count off!"

Alexis was standing between Nick and Ruby, which meant Nick was eleven, she was twelve, and Ruby was thirteen. Jackie, a certified, was number one, so she would guide off the edge of the crime scene tape. Max, number seventeen, was at the other end of the line, wearing the string pack. It was a giant roll of string that buckled in front and rested on the back of his hips. He began tying the string to the street sign. When they made the second pass it would serve as Jackie's new guideline.

Detective Harriman cleared his throat. "In addition to the knife, we're especially interested in footprints. The drag trail seems to have gone over the killer's footprints, effectively wiping them out. The guy who found her skidded down to where she was, which may have lost us some more prints. The girl was wearing boots with a round heel about two inches across, so that's pretty distinctive. We're not sure what type of shoe the killer was wearing."

Mitchell added, "Remember that we are looking for anything God didn't put here. It's not your job to decide if something is too old to be connected to what happened here last night, or even if it's evidence at all. Your job is just to find it."

Alexis and the others nodded.

"Okay, then." Mitchell raised his voice and looked in the direction of the TV camera. "Team forward!"

"Team forward," they echoed. Together, they dropped to their hands and knees, so that they were shoulder-to-shoulder.

"One entering grid!" Jackie called out as she crawled under the yellow tape. Ezra, who was number two, followed a split second later. In a few moments they were all under the tape and creeping forward. The rule was that you never got ahead of the person to your left, so the line they made was slightly diagonal.

Alexis's breath clouded the air in front of her. Anything in shadow glittered with frost. It was definitely still below freezing, but she was dressed in so many layers she wasn't cold, except for her hands. The chill even seeped through her leather gloves. At least Alexis had leather gloves now, and painter's kneelers. On her first evidence search, she hadn't had either. Afterward, she had to rub her fingers to get the feeling back. But leather gloves and kneelers were too expensive to buy, and neither ever showed up at Goodwill. A week later Jon had slipped her both, claiming he had found extras in the back of the equipment closet. They both had pretended to believe him.

Now, inch by slow inch, the teens crawled forward. Alexis's eyes scoured the ground. She was careful to brush back the leaves of larger weeds to look under them. She didn't want to miss something small, like a torn fingernail. Dirt, pebbles, small rocks, slightly bigger rocks, weeds, brown leaves, red leaves, yellow leaves, multicolored leaves. A snail in its shell, which she was careful not to crush as she crawled over it. In Portland, you usually didn't see snails, just slugs.

Beside her, Ruby sucked in her breath. Before Alexis could ask what was wrong, the other girl bellowed, "Team halt!"

Rubbing her ear and wincing, Alexis echoed "Team halt" with the others, and then straightened up. Her gaze followed Ruby's pointing finger. It had been drilled into them not to touch anything they spotted. Touch it and they became part of the official chain of custody.

Mitchell hurried up behind them. "Who called team halt?"

Ruby said, "Thirteen. Possible evidence."

Mitchell leaned down to look as Harriman came up. "What did you find, Ruby?" Harriman asked.

"A beer bottle cap." It was upside down, the inside flecked with rust.

"Flag it and keep going." Harriman sounded disappointed. It was hard to imagine that the rusty cap had anything to do with the dead girl.

Mitchell handed Ruby a small orange plastic flag on a wire, which she poked into the dirt next to the cap. By the time they were done, this lot would be dotted with dozens of flags.

"Team forward!" Jackie called.

"Team forward," Alexis echoed with the rest.

"Keep the line tight," Mitchell called out as they started moving forward again. "Shoulder-to-shoulder. We want a high POD." POD meant probability of detection.

They ended up stopping every fifteen or twenty seconds. Nick found a yellow napkin from McDonald's. Ruby spotted some broken glass. Alexis called a halt for the lid to a coffee cup.

As she stuck the flag into the ground, Alexis glanced ahead. Her path would soon intersect with a blackberry bush, the one near where the police thought the girl had been initially stabbed. How many times had Mitchell told them, "Go where your grid takes you"? And "If you can't see through it, you have to go through it"? The saying didn't apply to tree trunks—even SAR hadn't figured out how to do that yet—but they had been told it did to black-berry bushes. A bad guy might be counting on you not finding his gun because you weren't willing to brave thorns.

Right before she reached the clump, Ezra found a cig-arette butt and called another halt. While Harriman was looking at it, Alexis was frowning at the blackberry bush. It was a four-foot-tall mass of canes studded with wicked-looking thorns at least a half inch long. How in the heck was she supposed to go through *that*?

Behind her, Mitchell cleared his throat. "Want some advice?"

"Um, sure." She turned. Mitchell's normally pale face had two high spots of color.

He dropped to his knees behind her. "Tuck your chin

down and push forward and down." He demonstrated, butting his head against the air. But he was a little too enthusiastic and ended up bumping his helmet against her butt. Nick giggled. Face flaming, Mitchell got to his feet.

Alexis eyed the canes dubiously. "It still seems like I'm going to get all scratched up."

He shook his head. "I know we always say 'go through,' but when you've got an established clump like this, you don't want to try to wade through it. If you do, it will take you forever and you probably *will* get scratched. What you want to do is go over or under. And since we're looking for a knife, it's much more likely it is going to be on the ground. So you need to go under, where the evidence will be. You don't want to just push vegetation down onto your evidence and hide it more." He flattened the air with his hands. "I once saw a guy literally step on a shotgun and not realize it because of everything he was pushing down on top of it."

"So I go under," Alexis repeated doubtfully. She imagined the thorns raking her back, ripping through her Gore-Tex jacket. Which hadn't been cheap, even at a thrift store.

"Once you get under, there's more space than you might expect. Just think of the helmet as your battle armor. It actually does a pretty good job of getting you in there. Use it to shove yourself in as far as you can physically go. Then you literally just lift the whole mass of vines across your back." Mitchell lifted his open hands and pushed them over his shoulders. "There's a reason we've been called the 'forest eradication team.'" He let out a laugh that squeaked at the end.

"Since you already know how to do it, maybe you should be the one." Alexis liked this idea so much that she started to get to her feet so they could trade places.

Mitchell tugged her back down. "You've got to learn sometime."

Before she could think of a way to get out of it, Jackie was yelling "Team forward!" again and Alexis was echoing it.

Shoulders hunched, using her helmet like a battering ram, she started to push her way into the vines. A thorn scratched her cheek, reminding her to tuck her chin and to hunker even closer to the ground. She wasn't really on her hands and knees, but in nearly a fetal position on her forearms and shins, the ground just inches from her face. It felt too close, as if she were smothering. Alexis resisted the urge to stand and instead inched her way forward until she could go no farther. Then she reached up the way Mitchell had said to—silently thanking Jon for her gloves—and pushed at the mass of vines, scraping them farther down her back.

She had created a little hollow space, a kind of tunnel, below the fresh growth. Was this how a rabbit felt when it hid from a dog or a coyote? The sound of her own breath echoed in her ears, and the smell of dirt filled her nostrils. Light leaked in, and to ease her sense of claustrophobia, Alexis risked tilting her face up toward the patchwork of blue.

And then she saw it. Snagged on the vines about two feet off the ground.

A woman's mitten. Hand-knit, purple-and-white-striped. Turned half inside out. As if a bramble had snagged it and yanked it off.

But why would anyone get so close to a blackberry bush in winter, when there were no berries to make the risk worth it? And why hadn't the mitten's owner noticed it had been pulled off and retrieved it?

Unless it had been night. Night and she had been running through this vacant lot. Trying to get away.

Trying—and failing.

NOT SOME RANDOM GUY

NICK WATCHED THE WRINKLES IN Harriman's face get even deeper after Alexis pointed at the mitten. Judging by his expression, it had to have been the victim's. If Nick had just been two feet farther over, it would have been him who found it. Not Alexis.

In a low voice, Harriman conferred with Mitchell and Jon, then Mitchell clapped his hands. "Okay, everyone, we're going to break for lunch. You can eat between the two crime scene tapes, but don't talk to the media unless I'm there."

Harriman cleared his throat. "And I know some of you will be calling home or texting or whatever on your break. Remember that this is an active investigation. You can't say anything about who the victim was, you can't say she was alive when she was first found, you can't say she was stabbed. You can't even say she was a she. You know the rules. Even once it's been officially released to the media, you can only talk about what they've already reported.

Nothing more." His hand cut through the air. "No further details."

By the time Nick got to the sack lunches, all the ones with "ham" scribbled on them were gone. He reached for the last turkey, but Colton snatched it up with a triumphant grin. Great. All that was left was vegetarian. Nick did not see the point in refusing to eat meat. Prey and predator. It was a fact of life.

From his sack lunch, Nick pulled out the bag of chips— plain, which was more bad luck, because he saw other people with Doritos—and began to chomp away. While they had been searching, the crowd of onlookers had grown. They watched intently as Harriman photographed the mitten, first close up and then from a distance.

Nick spotted a familiar face at the far end of the crime scene tape. Kyle. He walked over, conscious of the stares and holding his head a little higher because of them. For once, he didn't even mind the helmet.

"Hey, Kyle, what are you doing here? Aren't you supposed to be at work?" He ducked under the tape and they moved off to one side. Heads turned in their direction. A barrel-chested guy in his midthirties was making a show of not listening.

Kyle kept his eyes on Harriman. "We've never had a murder in our neighborhood before. I decided to come over on my lunch break."

"You won't have much of a break, getting here and back." It was at least a ten-minute drive one-way.

Shrugging, his brother took off his cap and smoothed back his hair before replacing it. His curls were darker and looser than Nick's. People sometimes thought he was Italian. Not like Nick, with his light Afro that mostly just confused people. Sometimes they even asked, "What *are* you exactly?" with a tone that implied he was a different species.

Wilson, where Nick went to school, was mostly white, with some Hispanic and Asian kids thrown in. He and Kyle had gone to grade school in a poorer but more diverse part of town, while their mom had saved every spare penny. Finally, the summer before Nick entered sixth grade, she had been able to buy a tiny house in Southwest Portland, which had better schools and less crime.

At his new middle school, Nick started day one knowing nobody, since all his friends were across the river in a different school. He was skinny, he couldn't sit still, and he didn't look like everyone else. The other kids, who wanted to prove that they *did* fit in, made him a target. That first year, he was called names, spit on, pushed around. One kid stuck gum in his hair. His mom ended up just cutting it out, so his crazy curls looked even crazier. Another kid shot staples at him with a rubber band. Nick never knew if it was because of the color of his skin or because he was a stranger or because of who he was underneath those superficial things. Maybe for all those reasons.

During his time at Wilson, Kyle seemed to fit in far better than Nick ever would. He was a pretty good athlete, and he always had a girlfriend or two. He didn't worry, didn't get upset, didn't seem to care that much about anything. Maybe that was why even though he was new, too, he never seemed to get picked on. No fun in teasing someone who didn't care.

When trying to keep his head down didn't work, Nick had started getting louder. He looked for ways to gain attention. He clowned around, imitated teachers, and made jokes and faces in class. He wrote stories set in Iraq about heroic soldiers battling overwhelming odds. In his notebooks, he drew battle scenes and bits from horror movies and showed them around, heartened by any reaction, good or grossed out.

But nothing Nick had ever done had gotten Kyle's attention. Not until now, anyway.

Leaning in, Kyle said in a low voice, "So have you guys found anything interesting besides that mitten? Any clues? I tried asking one of the cops, but he wouldn't say anything."

"You know I can't tell you that." Nick took a bite of his cheese sandwich, which suddenly tasted better. In the weeks since he had joined SAR, how many times had he told Kyle he wasn't allowed to talk about anything they did that was crime-related? And how many times had Kyle not even asked him a single question, seemed to not even be paying attention? When Nick had been itching to talk—after, of course, swearing him to secrecy? But now he really *wasn't* going to say a thing.

Kyle was undeterred. "Do they have any suspects? Do they know where she was before she ended up here?"

"If they know that stuff, they're not telling us." Nick rewound the conversation. "How come you know it was a she?"

Kyle shrugged. "I just guessed. Besides, that's a striped mitten. And no guy is going to wear a striped mitten."

This was his brother. Not a reporter. Not some random guy. Nick pulled Kyle even farther away from the crowd, then leaned closer. "You can't tell anyone, okay?"

"I won't."

"It *was* a girl. She was stabbed once in the back and then hit on the head, but she was alive when she was found. She died on the way to the hospital."

"Are you serious?" Kyle was finally looking at him, not the cops. "Did she say who did it?"

Nick thought back to what Harriman had said. "It doesn't sound like she said anything."

"Did you see her?"

"She was gone before we got here." He could see Kyle already losing interest, so he added, "I saw her picture, though." He looked over his shoulder to make sure Harriman was still busy. "The detective told me she lives around here, but she didn't look familiar to me."

"What did she look like?"

"Pretty. Twenty-two or so. White with dark curly hair. High cheekbones and her chin kind of came to a point."

Kyle went still. "Wait—what was her name?"

"He didn't say. Why? Do you know her?" She did sort of sound like Kyle's type. Pretty was a given, but most of his girlfriends had also been white with dark hair.

His brother started to open his mouth. But before he could say anything, a wail cut through the air.

They turned. A cop grabbed the arm of a woman with frizzy, graying hair just as she tried to go through the crime scene tape. Even as they struggled, she didn't stop screaming. A second cop hurried over and grabbed her other arm, and she fell to her knees. She was wearing jeans and a purple ski jacket. Her lips were pulled back, her mouth open, her eyes slitted from the force of her screams.

She looked crazy.

But the words coming out of her mouth made perfect sense.

"My baby! Oh my God, my baby died here!"

PINNED IN PLACE

THE ONLY PERSON NICK COULD SEE MOVING was the TV cameraman. He was filming the grieving mother. The other onlookers had frozen at the sound of the woman's anguished screams. Some watched her helplessly, while others looked away, wincing. Even the cops restraining her looked like they had no idea what to do now.

Nick wanted to run over and kick the TV guy in the crotch and then break his camera. But like everyone else, he was pinned in place as shriek followed shriek with barely a pause for breath. It was like listening to someone being tortured. Kyle was biting his lip so hard that it had turned white.

Alexis was the one who broke the terrible spell. She hurried up to the woman and dropped to her knees in front of her. Speaking in a low but urgent voice, she wrapped her arms around the older woman.

Nick couldn't believe it. Alexis always held herself back. Even though she was friends with him and Ruby, she never shared anything personal. She didn't even like getting her hands dirty, which was pretty ironic for a SAR volunteer. But here she was, calmly beholding naked grief and pain. And unlike the rest of them, she had moved toward it. Embraced it.

What kind of girl was Alexis Frost that she could do that? Take the agony of an adult and let it fall on her own slender shoulders?

Whatever Alexis was murmuring in the older woman's ear, it was enough that the woman was able to pull herself together. First the screams were replaced by ragged breaths. Then the woman wiped her face on her sleeve. Finally, Alexis and one of the cops helped her get to her feet. She was quiet now, her face red and wet and raw. Half supporting her, the cop led her away.

The onlookers who had gathered along the crime scene tape began to talk again, but their voices were subdued now, their expressions more serious. It was no longer such a spectator sport.

Mitchell broke the quiet by clapping his hands and calling the searchers back in.

"I've got to go, Kyle."

Pulling his phone from his pocket, his brother checked the time and swore. "And I've got to bounce."

Nick ducked back under the two crime scene tapes and joined the others. Mitchell got them all lined up in their places again, just past the blackberry bush where Alexis had found the mitten. Mitchell worked from behind the line, not ahead, so that he wouldn't leave footprints or disturb evidence.

As he took his spot, Nick eyed the area they would be

searching next. It sloped down toward the spot where the girl's body had been found. At the bottom was a small creek, about six inches wide. Parallel marks on either side showed how the width varied with the weather. This week had been mostly dry.

As he knelt, waiting for everyone to get into position, Nick looked up at the sky. It was bright blue except for a single white contrail. Portland didn't have many clear, cold days. If he had gone to school today, he might have been tempted to wear shorts, flip-flops, and sunglasses, just for the double takes and the laughs. It was doable if you topped it with a down jacket (which you stuffed in your locker as soon as you got to school) and didn't have to wait too long for the bus.

The air was sharp in his nose, and the trees were nearly bare. Thanksgiving was almost here. After the break, everyone else would come back to school complaining about having to see their boring aunts, uncles, cousins, and grandparents. They would talk about being stuck at the kids' table when they were practically adults, but they would also complain about having to make small talk with ancient relatives, about being forced to choke down brussels sprouts or baked squash. At Nick's house, like always, it would just be the three of them: Nick, Kyle, and their mom.

A lot of years, they just ate Thanksgiving at restaurants. His mom's relatives lived back east. At Christmas and birthdays, her parents sent him and his brother each a twenty-dollar bill and a card bearing nothing more than a signature. Nick couldn't even remember getting a present or a card from his mom's sister. He knew they didn't get along, for whatever reason. His dad had been an only child, and his parents were dead now, too. Nick realized he didn't even know if he had aunts and uncles on that side. If his dad had lived, Thanksgiving might have been different. Everything might have been different.

The team started forward, with occasional pauses when people found broken glass and bits of plastic and paper that had once held fast food. Jackie found a hypodermic needle. And this time, it was Dimitri who had to go through a blackberry bush, but he emerged from the vines without finding anything.

There was a rhythm to their slow crawl forward. It was almost hypnotic, staring down at the ground, at the pebbles and the mud and the plants that were each a different shade of green. They were only a few feet from the creek now. Under Nick's knees the ground felt slightly spongy. Even though this morning the vegetation had been frosted, the temperatures hadn't dropped low enough to freeze the ground.

Nick lifted his hand to move it forward another six inches. But something about it was wrong. He turned over his glove. The tan leather was stained a dark reddish brown.

Blood. Wicked up from the sodden ground.

Just like the stains on the bottom of Harriman's shoes.

He smelled it now, even tasted it, a coppery tang furring his tongue. Nick's stomach rose and crammed into the back of his throat. Saliva rushed into his mouth. His cheese sandwich threatened to follow. He swallowed hard, trying to force everything back down. Not again!

As the world began to spin, he closed his eyes so he couldn't see the blood, but his mind supplied a different image. The knife jammed into the girl's flesh, leaving the blood he was crawling through. He swayed, his shoulder bumping into Ruby's.

"Tense your muscles," she whispered as she pressed into him, pushing him back until he was more or less upright. "Tense the muscles in your arms and legs and trunk."

His head was as heavy as a bowling ball. Under his hands and knees, the ground felt as if it were moving. But Nick followed Ruby's orders. He forced his eyes open, ordered himself to move forward. If he called a halt now, said he was feeling faint, then Jon, Chris, and Mitchell might decide that between that and the vomiting, Nick wasn't cut out for SAR.

"Wait," Ruby said. "What's that?"

Nick put his hand down before her words registered. Then he realized what he had done. There were marks in the mud that looked like footprints. Only he had just planted his palm on part of one.

He lifted his hand.

"Team halt!" Ruby yelled. "Team halt!" They all sat back on their heels.

Maybe the marks were old, Nick told himself as Mitchell and Harriman hurried over. Unimportant.

"We've got tracks." Ruby pointed. "It looks like two footprints."

"This mud next to the creek is like a natural track trap." Mitchell sounded excited.

Nick wondered how many people had walked through this vacant lot. At a minimum there was the guy who found the victim, the cop who responded to the scene, and the EMTs. People who lived in the neighborhood might come here with their dogs, or kids might sneak here to smoke something. The marks could have been made by anyone.

Harriman pointed at a spot just past where Nick's hand had landed. "That's the victim's boot print, with that perfectly round heel." It was a circle about two inches across, and a fainter rectangle that must be the ball of the foot.

Overlaying it was a second footprint. But it was smeared now, because of Nick's glove.

"Did you touch it, Ruby?" Mitchell demanded.

Nick felt heat climb his cheeks. "It was me. I caught part of it with my glove."

Mitchell made a disgusted grunt.

Harriman swung his big head back and forth. "We need to look for more tracks. If we can find more, we can get a direction of travel for the suspect. That could change the search pattern. And if it turns out the suspect left at a different spot than where he came in, then that points away from him coming here by car."

Nick scanned the remainder of the vacant lot. No other bare spots of ground that he could see. They had gotten lucky once—until he had ruined it. They probably wouldn't get lucky again.

And it was all his fault.

CRAWL THROUGH BLOOD

RUBY WATCHED DETECTIVE HARRIMAN knead a prefilled plastic bag he had just added water to. It was one thing to read about the technique for casting tracks, but another to watch it. She and the rest of the group were waiting as the certifieds who were also experienced trackers hunted more footprints.

"I ruined everything," Nick said. He, Ruby, and Alexis were huddled away from the rest.

Ruby tore her gaze away from Harriman. Visual input was distracting. Once she began to watch something, she would often stop speaking, which seemed to bug people. "They still have a good portion of the sole." In her mind, Ruby retraced the shape. "Enough to guess what direction the killer was going. And maybe enough to match it to him later."

"I should have been paying more attention. If I keep losing it at scenes, they might ask me to leave SAR."

"Can they really do that?" Alexis asked, her voice catching.

"I don't know," Nick said miserably. "Maybe."

Ruby couldn't imagine giving up SAR. With all the evidence searches they did, it was as close as someone still in high school could get to working a crime scene.

"Who's going to crawl through blood and not react?" Alexis said.

"Not like that, though," Nick said. "All of a sudden, I thought I was going to pass out. And you heard about what happened last night."

"It's called hemophobia," Ruby said. All those hours editing Wikipedia for fun hadn't been a total loss. When the other two looked at her blankly, she said, "Fear of blood. It can cause a drop in blood pressure and heart rate. And that makes you dizzy and nauseated."

"But I wasn't *afraid*," Nick said. "I was more just surprised. That's all. Same thing with last night. But I obviously can't keep doing that."

"Some scientists think it's an evolutionary mechanism." Ruby's eyes were drawn back to Harriman. Now he was squeezing out white casting material—a thick liquid—from a bottom corner of the bag, the way Ruby's mom would use a plastic bag to squeeze out icing on a cake. Laying it down in a tight zigzag that spread to fill in the gaps, he covered both footprints.

"If I'm hurt or someone else is, then how is nearly passing out going to help me?"

Ruby got a little defensive, even though she herself thought the theory had its weaknesses. "Way back in time, like in a battle or something, fainting might have been the smart thing to do. If you look dead, you get left alone. Also, if you're wounded and the sight of your own blood makes your blood pressure drop, you might be able to avoid bleeding to death. And if those things worked, then you might survive to pass on the gene that makes you react that way."

"My brother gets sick like that sometimes, too," Nick admitted. "So maybe you're right. But it's one thing if you're a package handler at UPS. It's another thing if you want to join up."

"Tensing your muscles like I told you about can help raise your blood pressure. And I think it's like all phobias. The more you're exposed to it, the less it will happen. SAR's a perfect place for that."

Alexis shivered. "I hope you're wrong about that. It's going to be hard enough to help someone who's bleeding. I don't think I could crawl through dead people's blood on a regular basis."

"Well, she wasn't dead when she left the blood," Ruby pointed out.

"I wonder if the guy—or lady—who did it knew that she wasn't dead when they left her," Nick said.

Harriman was using the edge of a wooden tongue depressor to smooth the tops of the casted footprints. When he finished, Ruby rewound the last bit of conversation.

"I don't know if they knew she wasn't dead," Ruby said, "but I do know it was probably a man."

Alexis raised one eyebrow, which Ruby knew meant she was skeptical. "How can you possibly know that?"

"Because women like to kill at a distance. They use guns, or sometimes poison. But stabbing is up close and personal. Men tend to be more hands-on."

"Knowing it's a guy doesn't really narrow it down too

much," Nick pointed out. "That only rules out half the population."

"The next thing the cops will do is look at the victim." Ruby gave in to the urge to lecture. "If they can figure out why she was killed, then that can lead to the motive and ultimately the killer. So they'll have to look at her relationships, jobs, personality, what she liked to do in her free time, whether she used alcohol and drugs, whom she dated . . ."

"Why does it all have to focus on her?" Alexis crossed her arms. "It's like you're saying it's her fault."

Ruby shrugged. "In a strange sort of way, it is. The killer could have chosen anybody. But he killed *her*. Was it a relationship gone wrong? Did he stalk her? Or was it a crime of opportunity—wrong place, wrong time?"

"Harriman said she was only stabbed once," Nick said. "Maybe it could even have been an accident. Like he was just trying to rob her or something."

"Maybe," Ruby said, attempting to be diplomatic. "They have to look at all the evidence and decide whether the killer was organized or disorganized. If it seems like it was planned out in advance, they're probably organized. Organized killers are smart, don't leave evidence behind, and usually kill strangers who fit a certain type. Almost all of Ted Bundy's victims looked just like his ex-fiancée. And like Ted Bundy, the killer might have tried to persuade the victim to go with him willingly."

"Why would you want to go off with someone you didn't know?" Alexis asked.

"If he was dressed like a cop or a security guard, you might. In Bundy's case, he would hang out on college campuses with a fake cast on his arm and ask pretty girls to help him carry things."

Alexis made a shivery sound.

"So organized killers are sociopaths?" Nick asked.

Ruby winced. In sixth grade, a student teacher had told her, "Your face is always blank. You never look me in the eye. It's like you have no feelings, like a sociopath."

Worried that he was right, she had tried to reassure herself that she wouldn't grow up to be a killer. For one thing, she didn't exhibit what was known as the McDonald triad: She didn't wet the bed. She didn't start fires. She didn't torture animals.

And, of course, there was the fact that she had no desire to kill anyone.

Eventually, she had realized that just because someone could look you in the eye, it didn't mean they were good. In fact, some people could be really mean to you while looking you straight in the eye.

Like that student teacher.

"Not everyone who's a sociopath is a serial killer," Ruby said now. "But, yes, probably most organized killers are sociopaths. They know what they're doing is wrong, but they don't care."

"What about the other type?" Nick asked. "Disorganized?"

"They're usually loners. They feel under some kind of stress, and in response they kill someone without much planning or even thinking. Usually within walking distance of their home or work. They choose a weapon because it's convenient, and they don't make much effort to conceal the body."

"That just sounds—random," Alexis said.

"It kind of is. Sometimes they're disorganized because they're younger, or inexperienced, or on drugs, or retarded." Ruby corrected herself. "I mean, developmentally delayed. Since they usually kill someone close to their home or work, the victim may even know the killer. The fact that we haven't found the weapon points to organized." Ruby's words slowed. "But then again, if this had been planned, why didn't the killer hide the victim's body? Leaving her behind some bushes in a vacant lot—that's just stupid."

"But if they're smart, they probably know as much about this stuff as you do," Nick said. "Maybe they're smart enough to make it look like a completely different kind of person did this."

CHAPTER 23

K

MONDAY

BARELY ALIVE

WHEN HE OPENED THE FRONT DOOR, Maryanne ran to him. He scooped her up in his arms. She didn't care what he had done. She thought he was perfect, just as he was.

"Is somebody hungry?" he asked, grinning.

She twisted in his grip, making a querulous sound in the back of her throat.

He set the cat on the floor, ran his hand down her back, then went into the kitchen. Maryanne trotted ahead, tail pointing straight up with that little kink at the tip. He got a can of Fancy Feast from the cupboard, peeled back the lid, and set it down on the mat.

The house was quiet except for the sound of Maryanne eating. Part of him was still waiting for his mom to call his name.

Only a few weeks ago, as soon as he had closed the front door, "Kenny?" would have echoed down the hall. Even though he came home at the same time every day, she was always worried he was a burglar. It was why she kept a gun in her bedside table.

And in response to her nervously calling his name, he would have sighed and then walked down the hall. Perched on the edge of her bed and told her about his day after she muted the TV and pushed aside her quilting. Now the house was quiet unless he was talking to Maryanne.

His dad had left before Kenny started kindergarten. And since then, it had always been Bev and Kenny. Kenny and Bev. She had persisted in calling him her golden child, even though his hair had been brown for three decades now.

She always said he was smart. But he heard what the others said. That he was "slow." That he was "off." When he got held back and had to repeat fifth grade, she had said it was a mistake, gone wheezing in to the principal to complain. He remembered standing red-faced on the playground, hearing the others giggle at her size.

She had her first heart attack when he was a junior in high school, but she eventually returned to her job as a receptionist. Less than a year later, another heart attack left her too weak to even leave the house.

It was an old coworker of his mother's who had gotten him the job at Strickler's. Sticklers, everyone called it, because Mr. Strickler was so picky. The customers loved the quality, the exotic offerings, and the fact that Mr. Strickler would special order whatever you wanted. The employees saw another side of him. He would rage if you didn't clean up behind the customers, didn't swoop down on their crumpled Kleenexes and discarded Starbucks cups. Every shelf had to be perfectly faced, so that when you looked down the aisle, the boxes stood shoulder-to-shoulder, so straight you could lay a yardstick across them. And sometimes Mr. Strickler did.

Kenny blinked and shook himself. What had he been doing? He was still holding the lid of the cat food can. He rinsed it and set it aside for recycling. Later he would tuck it into the cleaned can and crimp the edges so it couldn't slide out and cut someone.

Cut someone.

Oh God.

He had bought his own produce knife, and he kept it sharp for work, but he had never imagined he would put it to the use it had been put to last night. He kept telling himself that. It had all been a terrible accident.

Today along the crime scene tape there had been talk about installing dead bolts, buying guns, and resurrecting the neighborhood watch. His neighbors were convinced there was a crazed killer on the loose. They attributed all kinds of powers to him. According to them, the killer must be strong and smart. Fiendishly clever.

They wouldn't have believed him if he had stepped in front of them and confessed every detail.

Kenny, that quiet guy who had lived with his mom forever? The guy who had never left even as everyone he had grown up with moved away? Even as they went on to college and girlfriends and wives and families, to new cities and new countries. Or at least new zip codes. That sadsack mumbler? The one who worked as a produce guy at Strickler's in the West Hills?

He had watched and listened from the sidelines. It

sounded like the girl had still been barely alive when someone found her this morning.

All night, when he hadn't been able to sleep, she had been deep in her own kind of sleep, only a hundred yards away. When he had left, he had been sure she was dead.

Looks could be deceiving. Next time he would have to be sure.

Only what was he thinking? There wasn't going to be a next time.

Definitely not.

ROLLER COASTER

ON THE WAY BACK TO THE SHERIFF'S office, the van was absolutely quiet. Some people leaned against the windows; others just closed their eyes and let their heads hang down.

Alexis stared out at the flat darkness pressing against the glass. It was punctuated by occasional streaks of light from a passing car. Only Bran could make her forget this day. Tonight they had planned to get together to study. After hearing about the search, he had texted, asking if they should cancel, but she needed to see him.

It wasn't just that spending nine hours on your hands and knees was exhausting. The whole day had been a roller coaster. The excitement of finding the mitten, and then later the horror of realizing just what Nick had crawled through. Despite his tough talk, he had almost passed out, and Alexis had felt queasy herself when he showed her his stained gloves. Her stomach twisting, she had checked her own, but they seemed to have been in contact with nothing more than dirt.

And then there was the moment when she had gone to her knees in front of the victim's grieving mother and gathered her into her arms. Alexis had reacted out of instinct, an instinct honed by years of experience. The older woman had been crying so hard it was like trying to hold someone in the grip of a seizure, wordless and primal. And the press of the woman's hot, wet cheek against hers, the sound of her ragged wails in her ear, had been all too familiar.

Alexis's mother was bipolar. Some people still called it manic depression. Which was certainly more descriptive. When she was in the grip of the depressive phase, she suffered the blackest of moods. Alexis had lost count of the times she had hidden the scissors and knives, or worried that shoelaces and bathrobe ties might be too tempting, or the times she had held her mother while she cried. Or grabbed her hands when she beat her fists against her own head.

"You are the only reason I even bother to stay alive," her mother had told her during one of her dark times, her face red and twisted and wet from weeping. "If I'm not your mother, then I'm nothing."

That was one of the reasons why Alexis was careful to make sure that no adult ever found out exactly what her home life was like.

For one thing, what if the authorities separated them and her mom killed herself? And for another, who knew what kind of place they might send Alexis to? She had heard enough horror stories about foster care to know that anything was possible.

A few weeks ago her mom had been in a manic phase.

A whirling dervish, seeming to thrive without food or sleep. Barefoot despite the cold, she had insisted on blessing people in the park.

But after an involuntary stay in a mental health ward, she had come home with a crumpled brown paper bag holding a new batch of pills. Right now she was on lithium, Neurontin, Celexa, Klonopin, and a couple more drugs whose names Alexis couldn't remember.

The miracle was that so far they seemed to be working.

It wasn't as if her mom were cured. Alexis knew that. Cured was too much to hope for. The doctors never used that word or even the word *normal*. Instead they said *asymptomatic*.

Still, it was wonderful to be the kid again. To have her mom cook and clean and ask how school was going. To have her make sense.

Ruby's voice interrupted Alexis's thoughts. "You look very tired."

Alexis turned. Trust Ruby to state the obvious. The girl didn't have any filters. Last week in class they had practiced moving injured people. One of the sheriff's deputies had been playing mock patient. Ruby had told him, "You're too fat to lift easily," and not even noticed how the guy winced and tried to suck in his beer belly.

"I am tired," Alexis agreed. She looked at Ruby, really looked. Not just at her bright red hair and milk-pale skin, but at her expression, at how she was chewing her gum faster than seemed humanly possible. The other girl dropped her gaze. Trying to look Ruby straight in the eye was like trying to bring together two magnets with the same polarity. Your eyes just pushed hers away. "You don't look tired at all."

Ruby's face held a small, secret smile. She hardly ever smiled. She really didn't do much with her face. Unlike most girls, you couldn't guess what she was thinking—or what she wanted you to think she was thinking—by looking at her expression.

"It was an interesting day. Seeing that double perimeter. And I've read about that casting material, but I've never seen it used."

Alexis only nodded. She hadn't paid that much attention to either of those things, but she knew if she showed even a tiny bit of interest, Ruby would talk nonstop. When the van pulled up at the sheriff's office, Bran's small brown Honda was already waiting in the parking lot. After calling a good-bye to Ruby and putting her pack in his trunk, Alexis climbed into the passenger seat.

"It's so good to see you," she said. "Today was tough." Tears stung her nose. "Really tough." She waited for him to offer sympathetic words or pull her into a hug.

"Worse than yesterday?" He sounded skeptical.

"Way worse. I mean, for one thing, this girl was murdered." This morning, Mitchell had told them that even though Mariana had had to have surgery to fix her broken leg, the doctors still expected her to make a full recovery. "Today Nick actually ended up crawling through the victim's blood." She shivered.

"Oh." Bran started the car, looking straight ahead. "You still need to get your books, right?"

"Right. And maybe we could stop at Mickey D's?" She hadn't eaten much of her sandwich at lunch.

"Sure. Whatever." His voice was a monotone.

She finally focused on him. "What's wrong?"

"Nothing."

Thinking back to how he had acted last night, she made herself say it. "Are you mad at me, Bran?"

It took him a half beat to answer her, and during that space of time, some part of Alexis died. When he turned his head and his eyes finally met hers, they were blindly innocent.

"Mad? Of course I'm not mad." He turned back to the street, signaled, and then pulled into the order lane of the nearby McDonald's.

Maybe he was telling the truth. Maybe he wasn't mad. But he was definitely *something*.

He ordered a double hamburger, large fries, and a large chocolate shake. Alexis mentally counted her money and decided to get two things from the dollar menu. He didn't protest when she dropped the two dollars into his lap. He didn't do anything, including look at her. Or talk to her. All he did was pull forward to the pickup window.

Alexis tried again. "But it sort of seems like you're not here. Like you're thinking about something else. You were the same way last night."

The cashier slid open the window and Bran handed over the money, then he gave Alexis the bag. "I've got a lot of things on my mind."

"Like what?" She kept her voice bright as she half unwrapped his burger, releasing the smell of warm grease, and handed it to him.

"Things." He pushed the word at her. "Why do you

have to keep asking? Can't you see I don't want to talk about it?"

It felt as if he had slapped her. "Maybe you should just take me home, then."

"Maybe that's a good idea."

Alexis hadn't known Bran long, but she had thought she knew him. But the guy she knew wouldn't act like this. They rode in silence. Alexis tried to keep her breathing quiet, even as it hitched in her chest. She left her food in the bag. She wasn't hungry anymore. Bran's hamburger was in his lap, but he wasn't eating, either. A week ago they had fed each other french fries.

When he stopped in front of her building, she turned toward him. But he kept his hands on the wheel, his gaze on the road. "Good-bye," she said. In her own ears, it sounded like a question.

Bran still didn't move, didn't look at her. "Good-bye." It sounded like an answer. An answer she didn't want to hear.

She managed to hold back her tears until she put her key in the lock of her apartment. But as she turned the handle, she started to sob. Then the door swung open into blackness.

"Mom?" she called out, holding her breath.

No answer. But what was that in the far corner of the living room?

"Mom?"

The McDonald's bag fell from her suddenly boneless hands.

IT'S ALL BLOOD

DETECTIVE PAUL HARRIMAN SAT IN THE observation room overlooking the autopsy suite. Below him was the dead girl, the medical examiner, a pathology assistant, and a criminalist from the forensic division.

"Can you hear me okay?" Medical examiner Thomas—Tommy, except when he was testifying in court—Chapman looked at him over the edge of his surgical mask. Only on TV did pathologists talk with uncovered mouths over victim's bodies, spraying tiny drops of DNA-containing spit.

"Loud and clear." Paul took another slug of his twenty-ounce mocha with four shots of espresso. Now it was time to see what Lucy Hayes could tell them. IDing her had been straightforward. Her wallet was still in her purse, and the picture on her driver's license matched the dead girl. Maybe other counties did it differently, but here you would never have the family ID the victim. Too hard for everyone.

Lucy lay faceup on the stainless steel autopsy table. Both hands—the one with the mitten and the one without—were covered with brown paper bags, tied at the forearm. She was still wearing her coat, sweater, and bra, but they had been cut up the front and back by the paramedics so they could examine the knife wound and see if there were others. If Lucy had made it to the ER alive, all her clothes would have been removed there.

If, if, if. There were no more *ifs* for Lucy.

Tommy pressed a floor pedal and began to dictate into the transcribing machine. He reeled off the facts of what had once been Lucy: her race, sex, age, hair color, eye color. "Decedent is wearing a thigh-length dark blue Columbia parka, a black V-neck sweater, jeans, and calf-length black boots." As he spoke, the criminalist snapped photos.

After removing the bag, Tommy carefully examined her bare hand. "I don't see anything under her nails, but I'm still going to collect both sets," he told Paul. First he swabbed them, then he clipped them, putting the clippings into a test tube. With luck, there had been a struggle and she had scratched tiny fragments of tissue from her killer's skin.

Paul leaned forward to speak into the mic. "How long do you think we'll have to wait for test results?"

"Two days, three at the outside," Tommy said. Before moving on to her other hand, he changed gloves and got a new test tube so he wouldn't transfer DNA from one part of her body to another. Later he would take a blood sample so Lucy's own DNA could be ruled out from whatever the crime lab found. Her single mitten went into its own evidence bag.

Next Tommy and the assistant took off Lucy's clothes, rolling her from side to side. The back of her clothing was soaked with blood, and Tommy noted the holes in her jacket and shirt from the knife. The assistant put each item in its own paper bag, stapled it, and labeled it with the case number.

Her clothes would go to the crime lab to be examined for trace evidence, particularly touch DNA. Back when Paul started, DNA tests had required a bloodstain at least the size of a dime. Now all it took was about a hundred cells—the same amount left behind in a single fingerprint. And if you happened to be dragging someone, you were leaving behind far more than a hundred cells. Paul just hoped the killer hadn't been wearing gloves. Of course, the lab might find DNA from three people: the victim, the per-petrator, and the boyfriend. The last two of which might be the same thing.

The sad truth was, the first place you looked for mur-der suspects was among friends and family.

Before Tommy opened up the body, he X-rayed it. Paul hoped they might find the tip of the knife broken off inside her, but there was nothing unusual on the films.

When Tommy turned on the saw and made the Y-incision in her torso, Paul didn't look away. Didn't even blink. The only time he was no good at remaining detached was when the victim was a baby.

None of them was very good at that.

Fifteen minutes later a voice behind him made him jump. "Pretty girl. What a waste." It was his partner, Rich Meeker, dapper in black pants, a dark gray silky shirt, and a charcoal tie. Trust Rich to look past the blood and bones to see only the surface.

Yesterday while Paul had been with SAR, Rich had been assigning officers to search nearby Dumpsters, canvass the neighbors, and locate any neighboring security cams. The officers had knocked on dozens of doors to ask what anyone saw, heard, suspected. A couple had worked the perimeter to see if any of the onlookers had noticed anything the night before. One cop was even now hunkered down in a civilian's house that overlooked the vacant lot, watching in case the killer returned.

"Tommy tell you the cause of death yet?" Rich asked.

"I can hear you, you know." Tommy looked up at them. "I won't know for sure until I take off the top of her skull, but I don't think the head injury was fatal. The knife wound seems to have been what killed her. It perforated her right lung. Ultimately, I'm guessing she died from a combination of blood loss, hemothorax, and hemopericardium."

"I don't even know what those last two words mean," Rich complained.

"It's all blood, basically." Tommy pointed at the body. "She bled on the outside and the inside. We found blood in the pleural cavity. That's the space between the lungs and the chest wall. And we found more blood in her pericardium, which is the sac around the heart. That blood stopped her heart from working well, and eventually the combination of all three killed her."

"What can you tell us about the knife?" Paul asked.

"She was stabbed once in the right side of the back. The wound is about five-eighths of an inch by four inches deep."

"So that's how big the knife was?" Rich measured a space with his hands.

"It's not that simple, unfortunately. The actual weapon could be longer if the killer didn't push it all the way in. And if she was moving, the weapon could actually be shorter than the wound. Since the margins of the wound are fairly ragged, I'm guessing she probably was moving. I'm not seeing any serrated abrasions next to the wound, so I don't think we're looking at a knife with a saw back. My best guess is that this one was thrust to its full length. In the US, most knives are single-edged blades, so normally you would see a wound with one acute angle and one blunted angle. But on this one, both angles look squared off."

"What does that mean?" Paul was having trouble following.

"Some knives have a short segment at the top where both edges are squared off. So it could be that the knife was pushed all the way in. One end was squared off by the noncutting edge and the other by the guard."

Paul tried to imagine it. "So he must really have pushed hard to get it so far up the blade."

Tommy shrugged. "Actually, once the skin is penetrated, you don't need any additional force to penetrate the underlying subcutaneous tissue or muscle."

"Like buttah," Rich said, deadpan.

Tommy was picking up the saw again, ready to go for the top of the head. Paul turned to Rich. "So what have you learned so far?"

"She was at a bar Sunday night around midnight, and it looks like she walked there. She even left her scarf behind. It matches the mittens. Bartender says she's a semiregular. Not really for the drinks, but for the karaoke." Rich offered him a grin. "You're going to like this. When she came in last night, she found her so-called boyfriend, Cooper Myers, already there—kissing another girl, Jasmine O'Dell. Lucy dumped their beers on their heads." He mimed the motion. "Big scene. The bartender threw all three of them out. He says they stood outside yelling at each other and then they all left, each walking in a different direction."

"Two suspects already," Paul said. This was starting to sound like an open-and-shut case.

"My money's on the boyfriend. He got caught, and he got mad. Plus women don't usually tend to carry knives." Rich tilted his head. "When this wraps up, you want to go see what Mr. Myers has to say for himself?"

Three hours later Myers had had plenty to say for himself. Just none of it useful.

Paul had begun by making small talk about sports and school, even the dogs they each had as children. Anything to build rapport. Then, while Rich watched a video feed from another room, Paul had Myers describe what had happened, over and over, without interrupting. He looked for discrepancies, overexplanations, and outright lies.

The only problem was, he hadn't spotted any. Which was when he had brought in Rich, the pit bull to his sheepdog. Rich would never smack a suspect, but the suspect didn't need to know that. In search of the truth, you were allowed to tell all kinds of lies.

Now Rich was pacing the length of the interrogation room, which held nothing but a plain wooden table, a wooden chair, and a rolling office chair. Myers had the wooden chair, so he couldn't go anyplace. Sensing the moment was right, Paul rolled his chair up so close he could practically kiss the kid. Close enough he could smell the sharp stench of his sweat. He had been crying earlier, and now he swiped his nose with the back of his hand.

Paul kept his voice soft. "You must have been angry that she had embarrassed you in front of everyone. Because I would have been. At times like that, I see red. It's like things happen and I'm not even the one who is doing them."

He was offering two excuses in one, but Myers just shook his head. "I didn't do anything to her."

"Why are you even bothering?" Rich slapped his hand on the table. "We've got a dozen witnesses who'll say they saw those two fighting, both in the bar and outside of it."

Paul continued on as if he hadn't even heard him, as if it were just him and Myers. Most killers wanted to justify or explain what they did. All you had to do was offer them that opportunity. "Did you show her the knife just to scare her? Was it an accident? Or"—he managed to say it as if it were even a reasonable possibility—"did she come at you? Try to attack you again, the way she did in the bar? And you had to defend yourself?"

"How many times do I have to tell you? I don't own a knife. I've never owned a knife. And the last time I saw Lucy was right outside that bar. We all walked off, but then I cut over and caught up with Jasmine. I was with her until three in the morning." This story of his had the benefit of providing both him and the other girl with an alibi. One that Jasmine, at least so far, was backing up.

"You were the last person to see Lucy alive," Rich pointed out.

"I'll take a lie detector test. I'll do whatever you want." His reddened eyes pleaded with them both. "But I didn't kill Lucy. I love her."

"Which is why you were running around on her." Rich snorted.

Myers raised his head. "It's not that black and white. But I'm telling you, I didn't kill her. I didn't."

Go where the evidence leads, was Paul's rule.

But right now, it didn't feel like they had enough evidence to follow.

SO HARD IT HURT

THWACK! KENNY'S PRODUCE KNIFE flashed down, revealing perfect pale green flesh. The produce knife Mr. Strickler had originally supplied him with had had a fully squared-off edge and a flimsy plastic handle that didn't even have a guard. Eventually, Kenny had bought his own knife from a kitchen-supply company, a knife that ended in more of an angle, giving him a sharp corner to work with.

He swept the browned trimmings from the end of the celery bunch into the garbage can. No, he reminded himself with a little frown, into the compost. Strickler's was no longer the only high-end shop in town. It had to compete with stores like Whole Foods. Even some of the rich people who shopped here were starting to ask if his produce was "locally grown." When, this time of year, eating things grown within a thirty-mile radius would result in a sad, drab diet of cabbage, parsnips, and rutabagas.

Most customers, though, didn't care if their fruits and vegetables were in season or not. They didn't even care if it had to be jetted in from another continent. If you were determined to serve fresh raspberries, you didn't mind if they cost six dollars for a six-ounce green cardboard container. You didn't blink at paying seven dollars a pound for out-of-season asparagus, the spears thinner than pencils. People who shopped here thought you could get fresh cherries and nectarines in November.

And you could. If you were willing to pay.

A woman's voice made him start.

"Kenny! Look at this!" A woman in her late sixties thrust a head of romaine at him.

"What's the problem, Mrs. Whiteside?" He had tried getting people to call him Ken, but it never took. A lot of the customers had known him for twenty years, and to them he was still the nice boy who worked here after school.

Only maybe he wasn't so nice anymore.

"It looks wilted. I can't serve my dinner guests wilted lettuce."

"There's a truck coming in with a new shipment, but it won't be here until tomorrow."

She frowned. Her lipstick had bled into the tiny lines that feathered out from her lips.

"Well, I won't pay for that. It's not even fit to be rabbit food."

He didn't point out that no one was making her pay for anything. Instead, he trimmed off the dark outer leaves until he was left with the pale green heart.

She made him repeat the process for three more heads. Once, she turned away from him, and for a minute, his spine stiffened. His hand clenched the handle of the knife so hard it hurt, despite his calluses. How would she act if she knew what he was capable of? Would she continue to treat him so dismissively?

She took the lettuce without even saying thank you. He was a fixture. About as human as the silver metal cart he pushed between his displays.

Ah, but the displays. Even if people didn't notice him, they did notice his displays. When he was a kid, he had wanted to be an artist. And he was, in a way. Everyone said his produce displays were like works of art, contrasting colors and shapes. He had even seen people take out their phones and snap photos.

Today a silver bowl of orange kumquats sat in front of a mound of purple cabbages. On one side, zucchini were lined up in neat rows. Not a one marred by a fingernail mark. On the other side, plump Meyer lemons glowed like suns.

The night it had happened, he had been here late rearranging things, playing with colors and shapes until it all just seemed right. The store had closed, but he had stayed behind, shifting items, trying color combinations, placing baskets and boxes to add visual interest.

Now he brought his knife down again, exposing the beautiful white swirls within the head of purple cabbage. Did everything have a secret heart?

CLUE AWARE

WHEN SHE CAME HOME MONDAY NIGHT, Alexis had found her mom in a corner, rocking on her hands and knees, whimpering. At first, Alexis had been afraid someone had hurt her. Then she had realized that the pain was inside her mom.

How long had it been since Alexis had made sure she was taking her pills? At least a week, maybe more. She had been too caught up in herself. Selfish, selfish.

Finally, she had managed to get her mom into bed. And that was where she had been ever since. She slept and she cried, and sometimes she cried in her sleep. She got up only to go to the bathroom, shuffling down the hall, her head hanging like a heavy flower on a broken stem.

In the past few days Alexis had forced her to start taking her meds again. Made her open her mouth and stick out her tongue to make sure they were gone. But they didn't seem to be working. At least not yet.

On Wednesday, Alexis came home from school and found the apartment dark. It was clear her mom hadn't been up. She let her eyes adjust and then walked back to her mom's room.

"Mom?" She stood in the doorway. She heard the sound of breathing, so her mom was still alive. Everything her mom could use to kill herself was now locked up in an old metal toolbox. Alexis kept the key in her pocket. "Mom?" she repeated.

"What?" Her mom sounded like she was being forced to talk.

"Did you get up at all today? Did you eat?"

No answer.

"How about if you take a shower? I bet that will make you feel better."

"No!" It was almost a shout. Then her mom added in a softer voice, "I don't like the water. It scares me." She sighed. "I'm sorry, baby. I know I should be taking care of you, not the other way around."

Alexis nodded without saying anything. She didn't know whether to be sad or angry or worried. They had been down this road before. Many times. But would there come a time when her mom wouldn't return?

Three hours later Alexis walked into the sheriff's office for SAR class. New recruits had to attend every class, and certifieds were expected to attend as many as they could to refresh their knowledge and to add the voice of experience.

After waving hello to the deputy behind the bullet-proof glass, Alexis walked back toward the meeting room, where she settled in between Nick and Ruby.

"That's a big sigh," Nick said. "You okay?"

Alexis hadn't even been aware she'd made a sound.

"I'm fine. Just a little tired." She never talked about her mom. It was too embarrassing. Too personal. Plus all the adults in this room were mandated first reporters for child abuse, and child abuse also covered child neglect. Alexis didn't know if it mattered that she was sixteen now, and she wasn't about to find out. So far, keeping quiet had kept her out of a foster home.

The only person who knew the truth was Bran. The thought made Alexis sigh again. She didn't know what was wrong between them, or how much was her fault. She only knew that she had texted him twice since Sunday and he hadn't answered either time. Fine. She didn't need to be hit over the head. For whatever reason, he didn't like her anymore.

Jon stepped to the front of the room. "Tonight we're going to be talking about clues. There are five types of search clues. Can you think of one type?"

"Things you find?" Max said. "Like stuff they dropped?"

"That's right." Jon wrote "Clue Types" on the whiteboard and then added "physical" under it. "That also includes footprints or other marks left behind."

Nick's mouth twisted. He must be thinking about the footprint Nick had half destroyed. That and the girl's boot print were the only prints they had found in the vacant lot.

"What the people tell you," Dimitri offered.

Jon translated this to "testimonial."

"Documentary," Ruby said. "Like a summit log or a trail register."

"Someone's been reading ahead," Jon said as he wrote it down. Ruby's face turned nearly as red as her hair.

The other two types turned out be "events"—such as the subject flashing a mirror or yelling to get attention—and "analytical"—knowing that if a subject wanted to go from A to C, he would have to go through B.

Search clues seemed like the kind of things cops would look for, too. Alexis had been following the story of the dead girl online. Police had identified her as a twenty-one-year-old college student named Lucy Hayes. She had abruptly left a bar called the Last Exit late Sunday after getting into some kind of argument.

"Sometimes being clue aware means going that extra step," Jon said. "Say someone at a campground has gone missing. If you talk to the people in the tent next door before you even begin the search, you might hear that the lost person has been fighting with their parents. That's going to change the dynamics of the search in pretty important ways."

Alexis half listened, her thoughts bouncing from Lucy to her mom to Bran. She hated this time of the year, when the nights seemed to last twenty hours. What if she turned out to be like her mom, going from highs to lows, ricocheting between different kinds of crazy? Maybe Bran had noticed something she hadn't yet. After all, most of the time her mom thought herself perfectly sane.

"We have to be careful not to jump to conclusions," Jon said. "It's too easy to only look for clues that fit our theories and ignore those that don't."

Alexis shifted in her seat and caught a glimpse of Nick's latest drawing. A guy kneeling behind a prone woman. What looked like blood on the floor. He wasn't much of an artist, so she couldn't tell if he was drawing Mariana or Lucy or something straight out of his imagination. Of course, this being one of Nick's typical drawings, there were also arrows flying through the air and a dinosaur in one corner.

When class was finally over, Alexis walked out with Nick and Ruby. Someone was waiting in the lobby.

Bran.

Her heart started beating faster. She walked over, trying to keep her expression neutral. "Hey. What are you doing here?"

"I need to talk to you." It was hard to read his expression.

"Now?" He had hurt her, and suddenly she wanted to hurt him. "I'm kind of tired."

"Look, it's important, okay?"

Relenting, she said good-bye to Nick and Ruby and followed him out. He didn't say anything until they were in his car. But he didn't start it.

"I need to tell you something. It's about that callout on Sunday night."

"For Mariana?"

"Not so much that. It's what happened right after they found her."

"What— you mean when she got hit by that poor guy in the pickup?"

"Is that how you see him?" His voice was strangled with some emotion. Anger? "That poor guy?"

"I wasn't there, but from what Ruby and Nick said, it was an accident. He might have been going a little fast, but who's going to expect some kid to just run out in front of you?"

Instead of answering, Bran sat silent. It stretched out so long Alexis was afraid to break it.

Finally, he said softly, "Do you remember I told you once that someday I would tell you why I was in TIP? It's because I did something bad. Something terrible. And it's not something I can ever take back, or fix, or make right."

She absorbed this without saying anything. Bran? Something terrible? Those two things did not go together.

"Two years ago my parents got divorced, and we moved from Eugene to Portland. I started in the middle of the school year. It was tough. I didn't have many friends. That summer I got a job at Fred Meyer and I saved up enough to buy a car. This car." He slapped the dash so hard she started. "This same car. A lot of people can't believe I still drive it. But it's not like I can afford to get another one."

Alexis didn't ask why. She just nodded.

"See, all summer I had imagined driving it to school. How maybe people, I don't know, would think I was cooler if I had a car. On the second day of classes, I came over a hill. It had been dark at the bottom of the hill, but at the top, all of a sudden, there was the sun. Blinding me. Just when these two girls from my school decided to cross the street."

"Oh no," Alexis breathed.

In a broken whisper, Bran told her the rest. She saw it in her mind's eye.

Bran drives over the hill and into the sun. He squints. And then all of a sudden there they are. Right in front of his bumper.

No time to scream. No time to brake. No time to react.

A split-second later, the nearest girl and the car's bumper meet. A horrible, heavy thump rocks the car. Underneath Bran is the sound and feel of something caught and then let go.

At the same time, the other girl is sprawling over his hood. She slides up until she hits the windshield. It cracks under her weight.

Bran brakes so hard that she flies off the front of the car.

And then he is screaming.

He pulls open the car door, still screaming. Just a single word, over and over. *No. No. No.* They have to be dead. They have to be.

They lie sprawled about thirty feet apart. One in the middle of the lane. One in front of his car. Neither of them moving. Blood leaking from their mouths, their ears. It steams in the cool morning air.

He tries to find a pulse on the girl who had been on the windshield. His hand shakes so hard that at first he thinks he feels something. People have appeared, from where he doesn't know. Some adults, some kids from his school. Some run toward the girls, others phone 9-1-1, some stand stock still, their hands across their mouths, eyes wide.

One guy comes up to him. Bran thinks he recognizes him from his math class. "What have you done? You killed them! You killed them!"

He doesn't remember much about the rest of that day. But there was a girl from TIP, and she came and sat with him. She held his hand and gave him tissues and at one point he leaned into her warm neck and wept. Then felt ashamed for weeping, because why was he allowed to cry when these two girls could never cry again?

By the time Bran was finished with his story, Alexis was crying, too, but he was dry-eyed.

"There were a lot of rumors going around. They still go around, in fact. That I was drunk. That I was texting. That I knew one of the girls and meant to hit her. They call me a killer behind my back. Sometimes to my face. It doesn't matter the police investigated and ruled it an accident." He makes a sound like a laugh. "Sometimes it doesn't even matter to me. Because I can think of a million things I could have done so that it didn't happen. So that's why I volunteer for TIP. And that's why I've been acting strange. Because what happened Sunday night, that guy in the pickup hitting the little girl, brought it all back."

Instead of saying something, Alexis pulled him close.

CHAPTER 28
PAUL
THURSDAY

DNA DOESN'T LIE

"THIS CAN'T BE RIGHT," PAUL SAID, LOOKING up from the crime lab's printout that Rich had just triumphantly slapped in front of him. "I know this kid."

Rich was practically dancing in Paul's cubicle. "DNA doesn't lie, my friend. You trying to tell me that it's just a coincidence? Someone you already *know* was in the area at the same time the victim was killed, and now his DNA profile turns up under her nails?"

"But it's not his full profile."

Rich stopped his jitterbugging long enough to shrug. "We can get a court order and get that taken care of pretty quick."

Paul waited until Rich left to call the lab. "Can you just walk me through this? I'm still kind of confused by the results."

"I can do that," said Gunther Schmidt, the DNA specialist. He had a precise way of speaking, perhaps because he was a scientist, or maybe because his native tongue was German. "The only DNA we found on the brick belonged to the victim. Same for her clothing items. We did find male DNA on the clippings and swabs from her right hand."

Paul pictured it. The same hand that had lost the glove. She must have fought with her killer.

"The quantity of male DNA was very small. It was masked by the female DNA on her hands."

Paul nodded, even though the other man couldn't see him. That all made sense. It was Lucy's hand, after all.

"To allow us to focus on just the male DNA," Gunther continued, "we ran a newer test. It's called Y-STR typing. Remember, only males have the Y chromosome."

"Uh-huh." Paul closed his eyes to help him concentrate. When it came to DNA, it was all too easy to get lost in the weeds.

"The Y-STR test looks at certain locations on the Y chromosome that are passed down undiluted from each man's father. Since it never mixes with the mother's DNA, it never changes except in the rare case of a random mutation. That means all the males in a family have exactly the same Y-STR profile: fathers, grandfathers, sons, uncles, brothers, and so forth."

"So my brother and my dad and me—there's a part of our DNA that's identical?" The idea was slightly creepy. Didn't you want to be different from your family, to make your own path?

"Exactly so." Gunther made a small chuckle at his own pun. "And under Oregon state law, we are now allowed to do a familial search if there is no perfect full DNA match in the system. So we found a match for the Y-STR from the victim's hand."

"So that means the person whose Y-STR matches did it?"

Gunther didn't bother to disguise his sigh. "Obviously not, given who it matches. But he is probably a relative. If he somehow had been able to do it, the DNA would have been a perfect match. The entire sequence is as unique as a fingerprint. One in 244 males has this particular Y-STR."

"So it's a relative?" Whether it was nature or nurture, Paul didn't know, but about half the people serving time had had at least one close relative who has also served time.

"At some point even two unrelated men who have the same Y-STR probably still share a common male ancestor. Until I have a complete DNA profile that I can match to what was found on the victim, I can only give you the numbers and the probabilities as to whether your suspect might have done it. You have to look at the totality of circumstances."

Paul thanked Gunther and hung up. Right now, this particular Y-STR test was a noose that was closing. Only Paul couldn't believe the identity of the person caught in it. Twenty years a cop, and he could still be surprised. He sighed. And he had liked this kid.

IF YOU WERE THE KILLER

WHEN THE PHONE ON THE WALL RANG, Nick's English class was taking a pop quiz.

"Must it be right now?" Mr. Dill said after listening to whoever was on the other end. "He's taking a test." Everyone was watching the teacher, praying that he or she would be the one. But it was Nick who won the lottery. "You're wanted down in the office," Mr. Dill said, adding when he started to leave, "You might want to bring your things."

It was even more of a surprise to find Detective Harriman waiting for him. He was dressed in a rumpled black suit and an even more rumpled trench coat. Nick hadn't seen him since the evidence search four days ago.

"Hey, man. What are you doing here?"

The office lady, Mrs. Weissig, looked from Harriman to Nick and back again. She was making no pretense of not listening.

Harriman pulled him to one side and lowered his voice. "I got to thinking about what you told me Monday. I talked to the pathologist. The time you were driving down the street was the time he believes that girl was killed. It would be good for you to come down to the police station and complete a witness statement for me."

"But I'm not a witness," Nick said, wishing he were. "I didn't see anything."

Harriman shrugged. "You could have seen something without even being aware of it, or at least aware of its significance."

What if he *had* seen a key piece of evidence? Nick imagined the headlines. Maybe he'd even get some kind of award.

"And sometimes *not* seeing something can be nearly as good as seeing something, because it can help us rule out certain scenarios. We need what you saw—or didn't see—on the record. I already talked to your mom so she wouldn't worry if you were home late."

Nick signed himself out, writing "consulting with police" under *Reason for Absence*. If only there were someone else in the office besides Mrs. Weissig to notice him leaving with a homicide detective.

As they drove downtown, Harriman said, "So this happened in your neighborhood, Nick. If you were the killer, where would you hide the knife?"

Six or seven blocks away from his house wasn't exactly his neighborhood. Nick didn't know every bush and culvert the way he would on his own block. Still, Harriman was waiting for his answer. "Maybe try storm grates? Or people's bushes?"

Harriman nodded, but they were pretty obvious answers. When Harriman was busy circumnavigating a slow-moving truck, Nick quickly texted Alexis and Ruby with one hand to let them know about the latest development. When they got downtown, Harriman parked in one of the spaces reserved for the police, and then they walked into headquarters together. Nick held himself tall as a few officers nodded at them.

Once on Harriman's floor, the detective led him back past a warren of cubicles to a blank, impersonal room. Nick had been here once before, to pick out the photo of a person the police thought was a killer. The room held a table and two chairs, one on wheels and one without. Harriman took the one with wheels. Nick sat down on the other and put his backpack on the floor between his feet.

Two brown cardboard boxes, about the size of small pizza boxes, lay on the far corner of the otherwise empty table. Each was printed with the word *Evidence* in big black letters. The preprinted lines had been filled with scribbled notes Nick couldn't make out.

"Are you chewing gum?" Harriman pointed at the wastebasket. "Because you can't in here."

"I'm not." Gum made Nick think of Ruby and her obsession with unusual gum flavors.

"Before we start, Nick, are you hungry? Thirsty?"

"I'm good." It was weird to have Harriman being so solicitous, but it must be because Nick was key to breaking this thing open.

Harriman looked at the phone in Nick's hand. "Would you mind turning that off while we're talking?"

"Sure." Nick set it to vibrate and slipped it into his pocket.

"So if you were this guy, how would you have killed her?"

Nick grimaced. "I don't know."

"Come on. Help me out. I've been thinking about it so much I can't even think straight. How do you think you would do it?"

It was kind of flattering that the detective was looking to him for help. Nick tried to think. "I guess I would go in low." He held out his hand, curled around an imaginary knife, and demonstrated. "Into her belly. And then up. So you could get past the rib cage."

"Remember, Nick, you're holding a knife. So why is she going to be standing facing you? No, she's going to be running away, isn't she?"

Nick was letting the detective down. "I don't know. Then in the back, I guess."

Harriman reached over, picked up the top evidence box and opened it. Inside was a clear plastic envelope, and inside that was a knife.

He slid the box toward Nick. "What could you tell me about a knife like this?"

GOOD FOR STABBING

NICK'S PULSE SPED UP. HE REACHED OUT a hand, pulled it back. "Oh, dude. Did you find that at the crime scene?" He didn't see any blood on the blade, but the killer could have plunged it into the earth or wiped it clean on his pants.

Harriman tilted his head and just looked at him from under his shaggy eyebrows. Nick realized he probably wasn't allowed to ask.

He leaned over it. "I've got a knife a lot like this. A lot." It looked like the combat knife Jon had told him not to carry.

"You do?"

"You know. For SAR. There's a million things you need a knife for out in the field. You might need to cut someone's clothes to get at an injury, or saw a branch to make a travois, or cut a rope or something."

"Do you think this knife would be good for stabbing? Like, do you think someone could have used a knife like this to kill that girl?"

Nick regarded it. "Maybe. But I think that jagged edge on the back of the knife—the saw back—would make it hard to pull it out." In history, they had just seen the movie *All Quiet on the Western Front*, which he thought might have been based on a book. In the movie, an officer had lectured a recruit carving notches into a knife blade, telling him it would make it harder to pull back out of the enemy.

Harriman was silent. Nick wondered if the movie had been wrong. He decided not to bring up the knife in his pocket. He didn't want to get in trouble for bringing it to school.

Finally, Harriman said, "Why do you think this girl was killed?"

Nick tried to think of why. "Did they steal anything from her?"

"Not that we know of."

"Did they rape her?"

"No. So why do you think they did it?"

"I don't know. They'd have to be sick." He imagined how awful it had been for that girl. Lucy. Running in the dark. Being stabbed. Being hit in the head. Being dragged. Being discarded like a piece of trash. Being left all alone as your life ebbed away.

"I wonder what you would say if I told you something, Nick." Harriman was looking straight at him.

"Told me what?"

"That knife doesn't just *look* like your knife." He paused. "It *is* your knife."

"Wait. Why do you have my knife?" Understanding dawned. "Do you think *I'm* the killer?" Nick tried to laugh, but it came out sounding broken. This couldn't be

135

happening to him. "I don't even know that girl. I was never anywhere near her."

"But you were, weren't you, Nick? You told me yourself that you drove down that street at the time she was attacked. And yet you claimed you didn't see her."

Harriman was suddenly acting like they were on opposite sides. But how was that possible? Nick was in SAR. He was going to join the army. He was one of the good guys. And Harriman *knew* that. His scalp prickled. "Because I didn't. How can you even think that? Why would I have told you that if I killed her?" His mouth was suddenly dry, and he forced himself to swallow.

Harriman seemed unconcerned. "Because you knew it would turn up. You knew we would look at footage from nearby security cams, probably see that you had been there. That forced you to tell the truth."

"So if I'm honest, if I tell you the truth, then that's just more proof that I'm lying?" He could feel his pulse in his temples and at the base of his throat, as if he had just run a mile. His phone buzzed in his pocket, but he ignored it.

Harriman kept on as if Nick hadn't spoken. "You drove down the street and what—you saw her walking? We know she'd been drinking and she was upset. Did you offer her a ride? Because it was cold? Because you saw her crying? Because you were worried about a girl walking alone at night?" He sighed. "And then something went wrong."

"I didn't see her, I swear it." Was the detective even listening? "I didn't see her, and I didn't hurt her."

Harriman's mouth twisted, and he heaved a sigh. "Everyone snaps. Everyone has a breaking point. You were coming home from SAR, all keyed up, you had your knife with you, you saw this girl, you offered her a ride, and she said no. Or she said yes and changed her mind."

With his deep voice and wrinkled face, Harriman reminded Nick of a pit bull. Weren't those the dogs that grabbed on and didn't let go?

"It wasn't me! I swear it! Bring me a stack of Bibles." This was like those nightmares where, whatever you did, however hard you tried to escape from the killer or the kidnapper or the rising floodwaters, it failed. Tears pricked his eyes, but he blinked them back.

Harriman heaved a sigh. "Look, I like you, Nick, I really do. If you tell me the truth, then I can try to help you. You're a minor. You may need counseling, maybe medication. Believe me, you don't want to get sentenced to adult prison. But I can't help you if you don't tell the truth."

"If you really liked me, you would believe me."

The words just seemed to bounce off the detective. "We have your computer. We know you searched for information about Lucy Hayes online, over and over. Trying to figure out what we knew. Well, I'll tell you what we know, Nick. We know now that you did it." Harriman's sad hound-dog eyes never left his face.

"How did you get my computer?"

"We searched your room."

Nick froze. What had they found? Did his mom know?

YOU'RE NOT FOOLING US

"I'M GOING TO GIVE YOU A MOMENT TO think about things." Harriman tapped the table with one hand. "And when I come back, you need to tell me what really happened that night."

Not trusting his voice, Nick nodded. He didn't know what to do, what to think. *Harriman believes I did it.* He knew Nick, had talked to him a half-dozen times, easy, and he still thought Nick was a killer. Even though there was an explanation for everything the detective had talked about, Nick hadn't done a very good job of making things clear. He needed to calm down. To stop freaking out about whether the police had told his mom about his stash of girly magazines.

When Harriman reappeared, Nick wasn't sure how much time had passed. There were two other people with him. One was a tall man with an athletic build. He looked Italian. The other was a young dark-haired woman towing an office chair.

"Rich Meeker," the guy said with a curt nod. "Homicide." He looked at Nick as if he were something he had scraped from the bottom of his shoe, then he leaned against the wall next to the door and crossed his arms.

In contrast, the woman smiled as she stretched out a slender hand. "Hello, Nick, I'm Officer Rebecca Hixon. But you can call me Rebecca." Something about her was familiar, but Nick couldn't quite place her.

He was not going to call her anything. When he shook her hand, he held it as lightly as possible. What if he squeezed too hard and she decided it meant he was aggressive?

She sat down in her chair. "Detective Harriman asked me to join you because he thinks he might have been overreacting a little earlier. He realized he needed another opinion. A more neutral one. He's asked me to help him figure out the truth."

Harriman looked down at the carpet and nodded. Maybe he had gotten in trouble for how he had treated Nick. Maybe someone on the other side of the camera Nick had spotted in the corner had told Harriman that he was crazy, that there was no way Nick could have done it.

"Okay," Nick said. He crossed his arms, then uncrossed them, worried he looked defensive.

"Let me start by asking—did you know Lucy Hayes?" she asked.

"No. He already asked me that."

"Have you ever seen her before?"

"No." But she had lived in his neighborhood. What if Nick was lying and didn't even know it? "If I have seen her, like in a crowd or something, I don't remember it. I didn't recognize her photo when he showed it to me."

She nodded. "Now, this girl you may or may not have known—"

Nick interrupted. "I already said. I don't know her."

Her gaze flashed over to Harriman, her face unreadable. "Anyway, what I've heard is that she had a thing for younger guys."

Was that true? And even if it was, would a girl like that go for someone like him? "Oh, right. Like a girl that pretty is going to be interested in me." Couldn't they see how ridiculous the idea was?

"We've also heard that she liked to tease men," Harriman said.

The lady cop nodded. "She probably went too far this time, flaunting herself, and just set some poor guy off."

"I've heard this girl was a fighter," Harriman said. "Take what happened in the bar earlier that night. She attacked some poor guy she was convinced was her boyfriend, as well as this completely innocent girl."

Nick stayed silent. Were they telling the truth about what had happened that night—at least as far as Lucy Hayes was concerned?

"I remember what it was like when I was sixteen." Harriman looked up at the white tile ceiling. "Women and girls all around you, but you weren't allowed to touch them."

"Have you ever had a girlfriend, Nick?" the lady cop asked. She rolled closer. Too close.

He wanted to lie, but did they have ways to check? "Not really. No." It wasn't for lack of trying. He had kissed a girl and maybe done a little more than that playing Seven Minutes in Heaven in the coat closet at Trevor Kennedy's party that one time last spring. But afterward, Lark Munroe wouldn't even look at him or answer his texts, let alone talk to him.

"Did something happen that night and maybe get out of hand?" she asked softly.

Nick had known there was something about the lady cop, and now he figured out what it was. She was slender, a couple of inches shorter than him, with shoulder-length brown hair framing a heart-shaped face.

It was no accident that she was in this room. She was the same general physical type as Lucy Hayes. Did they think he would snap and stab her, too, snatch the pen tucked behind her ear and attack?

"I'm not going to dislike you." She cocked her head. "Why don't you tell me what happened?"

Like he cared what she thought of him! Although part of him did care, or at least care what Harriman thought. "Nothing happened. I just drove down that block—that's all! On my way home from SAR!"

"Nick, come on, you're just fooling yourself." Her voice was soft, reasonable. "And I don't think that's working. Because you're not fooling us, that's for sure." She pulled the second evidence box over and opened it. Inside was a stack of pages. "We also have your drawings. They reveal a lot about you. About the way you think."

Nick's face flamed. It was as embarrassing as having someone walk in while you were using the bathroom. "Where did you get those?" he demanded.

"From your locker and your house."

"You had no right to do that!" Did Mrs. Weissig know? Because if she did, soon everyone else at school would.

"I'm afraid we do, Nick. We got permission to search from both your mom and your school." She picked up the top drawing and turned it toward Nick. It showed a woman, limp in a muscular man's arms, her head hanging back. "Look at this girl." She tapped her finger. "She's dead, isn't she?"

"No, she's not. He's carrying her because she's hurt." It was too embarrassing to say it was a fantasy Nick often had, a fantasy of being a hero. Of being big instead of scrawny.

"Is that how you carried Lucy? After you stabbed her?"

"What? No!"

"Then how do you explain this?" It was the drawing he had made Wednesday night in SAR. "A guy dragging a woman's body from under the arms. With blood dripping from the back."

"I was thinking about it. That's all. Trying to figure out what happened."

"Or reliving it?" She raised her hand before Nick could answer. "We found page after page of drawings of people bleeding and dying." She riffled through them. "Dismemberments, torture, stabbings, and shootings. Sometimes captioned with the person begging or screaming."

Nick drew scenes from movies or from graphic novels (although he was nowhere near as good as the real illustrators). Sure, sometimes his drawings grossed people out, but he didn't mind. Not if it meant they were paying attention.

But this was definitely not the kind of attention he'd wanted.

He looked from one face to another. Harriman looked sad. Meeker looked angry. The lady cop regarded him with twisted lips and narrowed eyes. When his mom looked at him like that, it meant she thought he was lying.

"None of you are here to find out the truth. You guys all think that I did it."

"It's past that time," Meeker snapped. "We *know* that you did it, Nick." He stalked over to Nick and started to raise one hand.

Nick shrank in his seat, but Harriman yanked Meeker back by the arm. Then he turned to him as if nothing had happened. "So why don't you tell us about it. Tell us what really happened. We're just trying to understand."

"There's nothing to understand, because nothing happened. I rescued a little girl with Search and Rescue, I drove home, and I went to bed."

Ignoring the other two, Nick stared right into Harriman's shadowed eyes. "How can you even think this about me? You know me! You know what I do. Why would I volunteer with SAR to save people if I secretly wanted to be a killer?"

"I don't know, Nick." The detective sounded weary. "Why don't you tell me?"

Nick gritted his teeth. "What? That doesn't even make sense. How am I supposed to explain something that doesn't make sense? If I killed her, then why did I help find evidence?" He sat back with a sense of satisfaction. Finally! Something they couldn't refute.

Harriman didn't seem rattled at all. "That's the thing,

143

Nick. When you showed up on Monday, you weren't there to help, were you? That footprint you planted your hand on, that was no accident. Did you do even more than that? Did you spot something you had left behind and pocket it?"

NOT DEAD

"NO! OF COURSE I DIDN'T TAKE ANYTHING at the search," Nick told Harriman and the other two cops. "We're shoulder-to-shoulder. How am I supposed to do that?" Something inside him dwindled. He could see how it looked. Who knew better than someone on the team how evidence searches worked?

"Nick!" The lady cop raised her eyebrows. "Don't be lying to us, now."

"I'm not! I'm not lying."

She scooted her chair even closer and put her hand on his knee. "We know that you did it, Nick. We just want to know why."

He stared at her hand. If he pushed it away, would she let him? What if she resisted? Would she take that as just one more piece of proof that he had done it? He closed his eyes, took a deep breath, and tried to ignore the light pressure of her fingers the way he was ignoring the continued buzzing of his cell phone.

"We know it's hard to admit it, Nick, and we appreciate

that." Her voice was softer now. Every patient syllable made him want to punch her in the face. "We know what happened, but we don't know *why*. And we're trying to give you a chance to explain. If you're sorry it happened, Nick, you can help fix this. If you explain, then we can understand."

She leaned ever closer, even though there was no room for her. Nick shrank back, tried to make himself smaller.

"Did you come up behind her?" She was practically whispering in his ear. "Did she fall? Did she trip onto the knife? What happened, Nick? I don't know."

"I don't, either. Because—" *Because I didn't do it*, he started to say.

Meeker stepped forward and held his hand in front of Nick's face like a traffic cop. "No! Stop! Don't give us any bull. Tell us what really happened."

"I'm telling you guys the truth. I don't know what happened."

"Nick." The lady cop's soft voice was full of disappointment. "Why can't you accept responsibility for what you did?"

"Because I didn't do it!" He lowered his voice. "And it's horrible being accused of something I didn't do."

"We're not *accusing* you of anything." Her mouth twisted in disappointment. "We already know you did it."

He took a deep breath, tried to calm himself. There was no way they could arrest him. There was nothing linking him to the girl who had died. Nothing. "I never touched that girl. I never even *saw* her. You should be out there looking for the real killer. Not someone who's going into the army."

"And what are soldiers, Nick, but killers. Killers with a reason." She tilted her head. "Did you feel like you had a reason that night? Did she give you a reason?"

"Stop coddling him." Meeker slammed his hand into his fist.

Nick shook his head. It was as if they all had scripts and they were going to stick to them no matter what he did.

"Did she turn on you?" she asked. "Did she not leave you any choice? Was she asking for it? Did you kill her because you were afraid?"

"It doesn't matter what I say to you guys." He ran his hands through his hair, his fingers snagging on a knotted curl. Everything had gone south so fast. He felt dizzy. "You don't believe me. What's the point?"

"Nick," Harriman said. "I just want to help you. Just explain it to me. Did you do this with someone? Is that why there was a brick *and* a knife? Maybe they stabbed her and made you hit her, made you help hide her body. It's okay, Nick. If you tell us who else was there, we can protect you. We can work something out with the judge if you help us out."

"But I didn't do it." He was nearly whispering

"Look, Nick. The evidence is too strong for anyone to deny." The lady cop ticked it off on her fingers. "Lucy Hayes was killed in your neighborhood. You've already admitted that you were there, on that very street on that very night. You collect knives. And Lucy was killed with a knife." Nick noticed it was "Lucy" now that she was no longer trying to pretend she was on his side. "We hear you like to play first-person shooter video games, extremely violent ones, ones where you can stab people for extra points! You draw women who are dying, people getting stabbed. Your teachers say you often draw during class when you should be doing work. They say"—she pulled a notebook from her jacket pocket and turned back a few pages—"that your drawings are frightening. And we had a therapist look at them. He said"—another pause—"that you were rehearsing the murder, as evidenced by your obsessive drawings."

Harriman leaned forward. "And you were the first person from SAR at the search scene. You showed up to grill me about what we knew before the rest of them were even there."

"Mitchell gave me permission to come separately. Ask him. He gave it."

"I already did, Nick. And he says you asked for it."

They had talked to SAR? Who had they talked to? What had they said? Did everyone at school and SAR know the cops thought he was guilty?

"There's something else, Nick." Harriman was speaking so slowly that Nick got the weird feeling he didn't want to say what he was going to. Which meant Nick *definitely* didn't want to hear it.

"We found male DNA on Lucy's right hand. The hand without a mitten. She must have fought with the killer. We ran it through the national and state DNA databases, and there wasn't a match. But Oregon does familial DNA database searches now. It looks to see whether a relative of a convicted offender might be a match."

He paused, as if expecting a response. When Nick didn't say anything, he continued, "Which is why we're talking to you now, Nick. Because the DNA we found on her matched your dad's. Obviously, he isn't the person who killed Lucy Hayes. But someone who is a close male relative of his did."

What the hell was Harriman talking about? He wasn't making any sense.

"Of course my dad didn't kill her. He's dead."

"Dead?" the lady cop echoed. "Your dad's not dead, Nick!"

MIXED UP WITH SOMEONE ELSE

ALL THE AIR WAS SUCKED FROM THE ROOM. He looked at the lady cop, at her smiling white teeth and flat eyes. Then at Harriman, at his crowded mouth and shadowed gaze.

Meeker grinned at him. "The apple didn't fall far from the tree, did it, Nick?"

"What are you talking about?" He barely felt the renewed buzz of his phone in his pocket.

Meeker answered his question with a question. "You know what I've learned over the years? Bad blood runs in families, the same as anything else. I'm talking about a genetic predisposition to violence. Like father, like son." He nodded to himself. "Athletic parents have athletic kids, artistic parents have artistic kids. And violent parents have violent kids."

Why was he looking at Nick like that? "But my dad died in Iraq. He got a medal."

Harriman's face changed. His eyes widened and he

started to open his mouth. But Meeker spoke before he could.

"Nick." Meeker shook his head with exaggerated slowness, lifting one side of his mouth as if Nick had just told a not-very-funny joke. "I'm not talking about what happened over in Iraq. I'm talking about your dad beating someone to death with his bare fists in a bar. And Lucy—Lucy had just left a bar. Coincidence?"

Everything inside Nick went still. It was like the world had suddenly turned to black and white. Still recognizable, but not right. Not right at all.

"What are you talking about?"

"Twelve years ago your dad killed a guy in a bar in Northeast Portland. He said something just snapped. Is that what happened to you, Nick? Did you just snap?"

"You're not making any sense. My dad was a soldier. In Iraq. You've got him mixed up with someone else."

"Your father *was* a soldier. That's true." Harriman leaned closer, his sad eyes never leaving Nick's face. "And a little over twelve years ago he was discharged. Two weeks after he came home, he killed a guy in a bar over what he admits was nothing. Didn't even know the other guy's name, but he still went ballistic. Left a woman a widow, two little kids without a father."

Harriman could have been talking about Nick's own family. But it wasn't true. It couldn't be true. "You're wrong. You're wrong! I've seen the medal my dad got. You must be talking about some other guy. Some other Don Walker. And he died over there. In the war. When I was four."

"No. He went to prison when you were four. Is that what your mom told you? That he died in Iraq?" When Harriman spoke next, his voice was so soft he could have been talking to himself. "Maybe he did. To her. After all, what kind of mom wants her kids to grow up knowing they're the sons of a murderer?"

Nick didn't answer. He was incapable of answering. With one hand, he braced himself on the edge of the table.

"You're saying my dad was a killer?"

"Not was, Nick. Is." Harriman's voice was oddly gentle. "He's still alive. He's in the penitentiary down in Salem."

His dad was alive? The room spun. Nick felt boneless. He turned in his chair, leaned over, and rested his head against the cool, fake wood of the table.

His mom must know. Had to know. Known and chosen to lie to him. But what about Kyle? The thing was, he could totally see Kyle lying. But his mom? She had never lied to him.

As they watched him, the cops were silent, letting the poison seep deeper into Nick's veins.

He had boasted about his dad. Daydreamed about him. Wanted to become him. Now they thought he had. Because the truth seemed to be that his real dad was the evil shadow of the man Nick had imagined.

"I don't understand. You're saying that my dad's in jail."

"Prison," Harriman corrected, his voice still oddly gentle. "He's in prison. Has been since you were four."

"So how could you find his DNA on this girl?"

"We didn't."

The lady cop interrupted Harriman. "But we found the next best thing. A few months ago Oregon started doing familial DNA searching. If it can't find a perfect match, it looks for people who share a big chunk of the perpetrator's DNA profile. People who share DNA are usually related. One test the lab ran looked at a portion of just the Y chromosome, which only males have. In fact, it never changes as it goes down through the generations. A grandfather has the same Y-STR as a father as a son as a brother as an uncle. As long as they are all descended from the same male line."

Harriman took a piece of paper from his jacket, unfolded it, and pushed it over. It was some kind of report. Nick's eyes skimmed it. It was full of numbers and letters he didn't understand.

RESULTS OF Y-STR DNA ANALYSIS:

In the DNA analysis detailed below, the following Y chromosome Short Tandem Repeat (Y-STR) loci were analyzed using Polymerase Chain Reaction (PCR): DYS456, DYS389I, DYS390, DYS389II, DYS458, DYS19, DYS385a/b, DYS393, DYS391, DYS439, DYS635, DYS392, Y GATA H4, DYS437, DYS438, and DYS448.

Y-STR examination is male-specific, as the Y chromosome is solely inherited by males. Regions of the Y chromosome are normally identical among paternal male relatives (e.g., parent-son, full brothers, grandchild-grandparent, etc.).

Y-STR STATISTICS:

The DNA haplotype obtained from the swabs (Items 1.6 and 34.1) is consistent with that of Eldon Walker (Item 8.1), and is found in 51 of 15,697 total individuals within the database. Applying a 95% confidence interval results in a frequency of 0.0041, which is equivalent to approximately 1 in every 244 individuals. This DNA haplotype would also be expected to be exhibited in all male paternal relatives of Eldon Walker.

"What does this have to do with anything?" Nick felt almost giddy as he focused on the last two words. "Who's Eldon Walker?"

"Your father," the lady cop answered impatiently.

"My dad's name is Don. Not El—" Only as he said it did Nick realize *Don* must be a nickname. "Oh." No wonder he had had trouble finding his dad when he googled him, eager for the stories his mother wouldn't tell.

Harriman spoke into his sudden silence. "Your father doesn't have any brothers, right?"

"What? No. Why?"

"And it's just you and your brother. And your brother told us he was home in bed that night. That he goes to bed early so he can work the early shift at UPS. Your mother confirmed it."

Nick thought of the empty bed, the kicked-back covers, and willed his face into a mask. He had to be careful. So careful.

154

Had Kyle done it? His stomach did a slow flip. How could he think that? This was his brother. Not a murderer.

Only that was what he would have said about his dad. That his dad wasn't a murderer. That he was a hero.

And Kyle had always been such a good liar. Good enough you could start to doubt yourself.

He remembered how Kyle had suddenly bolted from the room when their mom started talking about the sirens. The sound of him retching. Maybe it hadn't been the flu. Had he been remembering sinking the knife into that girl, still sickened by it?

Or had it been just the simple fear that he would be caught?

A CALCULATED RISK

RUBY CHECKED HER PHONE. AGAIN. BUT there were no new texts. It had been over two hours since Nick had texted her and Alexis that Detective Harriman was taking him downtown because he was a potential witness. Two hours since he last answered a text—and Nick lived on his phone.

Ruby already knew everything that Nick had seen Sunday night driving past the area where Lucy Hayes had been murdered: nothing.

So why would the police still be talking to Nick? Talking to him when he didn't know anything?

The only answer was that they must think he did know something.

Or, Ruby realized as time ticked past and Nick kept ignoring her, they must think he had *done* something.

Instead of going to class, she hid in the bathroom until the bell rang. Then she walked down the suddenly empty hall, past the office, and right out the front door. Ms. Peyton, the administrative vice principal, was just coming in as she was going out. Ruby took a deep breath and tried to think of a lie, but Ms. Peyton only nodded at her and walked on.

Ruby realized that everyone knew what kind of girl she was, so that was what they saw. The kind of girl who would never skip.

Did the police think they knew what kind of guy Nick was? Were there things about Nick that might make them think he was the one they were looking for?

Ruby ran down the list in her head. Nick had admitted to being in the right area at the right time. He routinely carried a knife. Judging by his doodles, he was fascinated by violence. And he was impulsive.

Ruby also knew that underneath the brazen, bragging Nick was another guy, one who was capable of unexpected kindness. Of acts of heroism even when it looked like all hope was lost. But the police wouldn't know those things.

Then she remembered the evidence search and how he had accidentally put his hand down on the only footprint they had found. She was sure Nick's dizziness had been no act. But the police wouldn't know that. From their perspective, it might seem that he deliberately destroyed evidence.

Driving seven miles over the speed limit—a calculated risk— Ruby headed to the Fred Meyer on Barbur Boulevard, where Nick's mom worked. She found her at register nine.

"Hey, Ruby, what are you doing here?" Mrs. Walker threw a smile over her shoulder. Her hands never stopped moving, sliding item after item past the scanner and then putting them in the customer's heavy black nylon bag printed with a logo, not for Fred Meyer, but for Trader Joe's.

The dissonance threw Ruby for a second. Then she gathered her thoughts.

"I'm here to ask you the same thing. Why are *you* here? Why aren't you with Nick?"

She frowned. "Why should I be with Nick?"

"Because he's being questioned by the police about that girl's murder!" Only when Mrs. Walker's customer—an old woman in mushroom-colored shoes—whipped her head around did Ruby realize she had forgotten to modulate her voice.

Mrs. Walker froze. "You don't understand. He's helping the police. That's all."

"And just what kind of help could Nick give them? He doesn't know anything. It wouldn't take them two hours to figure that out. Unless they didn't believe him."

The old lady cleared her throat, and with a start, Mrs. Walker started passing items across the scanner again.

"But Nick didn't do anything wrong." She put a rubber band around a carton of eggs. "So it can't hurt him to talk to the police. They told me they just needed to get a few things straightened out."

"You've got to put a stop to it immediately. Nick shouldn't be talking to them without an attorney. They wouldn't be questioning him for this long unless they thought he was a *suspect*."

"Nick?" Mrs. Walker laughed. She actually laughed. "But he didn't have anything to do with it. Nick won't even kill a spider."

Ruby ground her teeth in frustration. "But what if the police don't see him the same way you do? If they talk to him long enough, they could make him start thinking that he actually did. Juveniles are psychologically vulnerable to suggestive cues and coercion."

"This is my son we're talking about. I know what he's capable of. I know he didn't do anything. I'm not really worried." She turned to the older woman. "That will be $35.87."

"And I know that, too," Ruby said to her back. "And I *am* worried. Nick might start saying what they want to hear. You need to go down to the police station and put a stop to this right away."

Mrs. Walker bit her lip. Ruby finally seemed to be getting through to her. "The thing is, I can't leave work." She lowered her voice. "We've got a new manager, and he doesn't like me because I turned him down for a date. I think he's just looking for an excuse to fire me."

"Then call the police." Ruby held out her cell phone with the phone number already selected. "Call and tell them it's over, and I'll go get him. They'll either have to read him his Miranda rights and arrest him, or they'll have to let him go."

Someone behind Ruby cleared his throat. She whirled around. "Is there a problem here?" It was a skinny middle-aged guy with an elaborate black mustache and a red polyester vest.

"Family emergency," Mrs. Walker said. The manager looked from red-haired Ruby to blond Mrs. Walker. "Can I take five minutes after this customer?"

"You've already got someone else behind her."

"Then after that. Please?"

"This really isn't the kind of behavior I want you to make a habit of."

"I'm sorry." Mrs. Walker lifted her hands.

He grunted. "This once. But don't think I'm not making note of it."

Ruby wanted to fly down the freeway, but she kept to the same seven-miles-over-the-limit rule. She found a place to park and ran into the lobby of police headquarters. Just as she went in, the elevator doors opened and Nick stepped out.

He was holding his coat. Under the arms, his shirt was stained with sweat. On his feet were plastic shower shoes, the kind that prisoners wore. His eyes looked huge and frightened.

Ruby was opening her mouth when Harriman stepped out right behind him. His voice was pitched for both of them. "I know you, Nick. You can't live with a secret this big. No one can. It will eat at you. But the only way I can help you is if you tell the truth."

"You know Nick," Ruby said to Harriman. "And you know he didn't do it. It's not even logical."

"Who ever told you that murder is logical?" Harriman spun on his heel and stabbed his finger at the elevator button. The doors opened back up, and he stepped inside without saying another word.

"They wanted me to take a DNA test." Nick sighed heavily. "I said no."

"Don't say another word until we're in my car," Ruby said, grabbing him under the arm. Normally she didn't like to be touched or even to touch, but this was different. This was like giving someone first aid. Under her fingers, she could feel how he was shaking.

Once they were both inside her car, Nick said, "They took my shoes for 'evidentiary purposes.' When I said no to the DNA test, they just told me they would get a court order." His face changed. "That must be why Harriman asked me if I wanted anything to eat or drink when I first came in. I thought he was being nice. But he was probably looking for my DNA."

"Why didn't you just give it to him?" Ruby asked. "I mean, sure, *you* must have gotten *her* DNA on you when you crawled through her blood, but she was long gone before we got there. And the converse isn't true. There's no way you could have gotten your DNA on her."

"They said they already know it's at least a partial match." He wiped his hands on the knees of his jeans.

"Then they must be lying. The police are allowed to do that when they're questioning a suspect and trying to get him to confess."

Nick was breathing fast. "I don't think he was lying." His voice broke. "Ruby, I don't know what to do. I don't know what to think."

"But you didn't do it, Nick. Right?" Something about him made her doubt her surety.

"What if I blanked it out? What if—I don't know— what if I sleepwalked or something?" He knocked the heels of his hands against his temples. "I don't know what happened. All I know is that they found male DNA on her right hand, and they said that it matches my dad's DNA— and any of his male relatives. Which means me."

"Your dad? But he's dead. How would they have his DNA profile?" Maybe this was the proof that the cops were lying. Ruby was nearly certain that whatever DNA information the army kept on its soldiers, it didn't go into CODIS, the FBI's DNA database.

Nick put his hands over his face. "My dad's not dead. Not according to Harriman, anyway."

Even if the detective could lie, why would he tell such a cruel, bizarre lie to Nick? "If he's not dead, then where is he?"

"In prison. He's a murderer, Ruby. Harriman said he beat some guy to death. I guess my mom must have decided to start telling everyone he was dead rather than telling the truth." Nick let his hands fall. His eyes shone with tears. "And Harriman said whoever left the DNA has to be my dad or one of his male relatives. But he doesn't have any except for us. Which means it has to be me or my brother."

"Kyle?" Ruby had only met him twice, not enough to weigh whether he could be a killer.

"So that's why I said no to the DNA test. Because once it doesn't match, they'll know it's Kyle. My mom told them Kyle was sleeping when it happened, but when I came home, he wasn't in bed. He wasn't anywhere in the house. I don't know where he was or what he was doing. I do know that if he killed her, it has to have been an accident. If he did it, he didn't mean to. I have to talk to him first. Maybe—maybe give him a chance to run."

I WISH YOU HADN'T

A S RUBY DROVE HIM HOME, NICK'S MIND was whirling with images. Of being small and having his dad lift him in the air with big hands. Of Lucy's blood darkening his gloves. Of Kyle running to the bathroom Monday to throw up when the police car screamed by their house. Of Harriman offering him something that looked like a cross between a Q-tip and a miniature scrub brush.

Ruby broke the silence. "Did they ever read you your rights?"

"What?" Nick shook his head, trying to orient himself. His hands lay loose on his lap, but he could feel them still trembling. That lady cop had tried to say it was proof of his guilt, that he wouldn't be shaking and sweating if he wasn't guilty. Of course, he hadn't told her it was because he kept wondering about Kyle.

"Did they read you your rights?" Ruby repeated. "They have to if you're in custody."

"You mean that whole 'right to remain silent' thing? No."

"Then you could have walked out at any time. But they didn't tell you that. And judges use the standard of what the prudent person would think under the circumstances. Not what an uninformed, naive kid would think."

Nick roused himself enough to say, "Thanks a lot, Ruby."

"I'm not saying you're naive in general. I'm just saying you are uninformed about the law. Next time ask to speak with a lawyer. Or even your mom. If you're under eighteen and ask to speak to your parent, the law treats that as the same as asking for a lawyer. Either way, at that point all questioning will have to stop."

"Next time?" Nick swallowed hard, trying to will his nausea away. "There had better not be a next time. If there is, it will be because they're arresting me for that girl's murder."

"I'm afraid you're going to see them again. Just because you said no to the test doesn't mean they won't come back and force you to take it. All they need to do is write up a warrant and get a judge to sign it. It might take them until tomorrow. So when they show up again, don't talk to them. The only thing you should open your mouth for is to let them get your DNA."

Ruby seemed so sure of herself, and of him. "How come *you* don't think I did it?" he asked.

"I know you, Nick. And I can't see you coming home from a SAR mission and stopping to murder some girl you caught sight of. It's not logical."

"The cops are sure that I did it. And they took stuff

164

from my locker and my room. That means they've got stuff with my DNA. Maybe, I don't know, maybe they planted it."

"They wouldn't do that." But Ruby didn't sound entirely certain.

"You weren't there. They all think I'm guilty. Harriman, his partner, this lady cop. I mean, Harriman seems sad, but he still thinks I did it. And his partner almost hit me. Maybe he wanted to make sure that everyone else is certain, too."

Ruby pulled into his driveway. The house was dark. Nick checked the time on his phone. His mom was still at work. He didn't know where Kyle was. Maybe that was better. He needed time to think about what the police had said.

"Do you want me to come in with you?" Ruby asked. She didn't look at him.

"No. That's okay." Nick couldn't wait to be alone. "Thanks again, though, for everything you did today."

When he went inside, his house was no refuge. In his room, all the drawers gaped open. It was clear the contents had been taken out, gone through, and just stuffed back in the same general area. Nothing was folded anymore. Not that Nick ever folded anything, but his mom did. His socks and underwear, usually on opposite sides of the same drawer, were all commingled.

He imagined Harriman and his partner and that lady cop sifting through everything with gloved hands. Maybe holding up something particularly personal or embarrassing and laughing. It was like knowing someone had gone through your thoughts.

In addition to the magazines, all his notebooks, drawings, and his combat knife were gone. So was his computer. So were all his shoes. He lay down on his bed and put his arm over his eyes.

Ten minutes later the front door opened. "Nick?" his mother called.

He didn't say anything. Didn't move. He felt the bed shift as she settled in beside him.

"Nick, honey, I'm sorry." She touched the arm over his eyes and took her fingers away. "I just thought they would have a few questions, and you would answer them, and that would be it. Of course I wasn't thinking they thought you did it. That's a ridiculous idea."

Anger clotted his throat. "Oh really?" He couldn't stand to be so close to her. He sat up and pushed himself to his feet. "It's not so ridiculous knowing that my father is a murderer."

He heard her quick intake of breath. "I wish you hadn't learned it like that."

"And how was I supposed to learn it? You lied to me, over and over. You let me think he was dead!"

"I didn't tell you he was dead." Her face was pale. "I just didn't correct you."

"Then why did you bother to let me know the truth about Santa Claus and the Easter Bunny?" Nick's voice rose and he didn't try to rein it in. "You let me know the truth about everything *except* my dad. It was like poor little Nick, let him stay in his make-believe world." He made a sound like a laugh. "No wonder we never go visit any family. Because they might actually tell me the truth. And you know what? I'm old enough. I deserve the truth. My whole fricking life has been a lie. I wanted to be like him." He leaned down so he was in her face. "I wanted to be like him, and now that's exactly what they think I am."

"Listen, Nick." Bright red now splotched her cheeks. She blinked and tears rolled down her face. "You were four when he went to prison. Four. I did not lie. Not really. You put things together, and you thought you knew the truth. If I lied, it was more by omission."

"Oh yeah, like that really makes a difference." Tears burned his own eyes, but he ignored them. Why was he crying, anyway? He was mad. "Does Kyle know?"

Her long silence told him the answer. Finally, she said, "He was older. He remembered the truth. He remembered how terrible it was, the cops dragging your dad away, the reporters banging on the door and taking our pictures whenever we went outside." She took a ragged breath. "Why do you think I don't want you to join up? Iraq changed your dad. Before, sure he got angry sometimes, but it was nothing like it was after. I look at you, Nick, and there are times I see him. In the shape of your face, the way you hold yourself. He was hyperactive, like you are. Impulsive. Good, bad, good. He teetered."

"What? So does that mean you really think I did this thing? You think I came home from saving a little girl's life and right after that I stabbed some lady in the back and dragged her into that vacant lot to die?"

"No." Her voice got stronger. "No. I don't believe that."

But the thing was, Nick had heard the catch in her voice. The catch as part of her wondered if it were true.

167

"So what really happened to Dad? They said he beat somebody to death in a bar."

"He went out drinking. We'd been fighting. We'd been fighting a lot. It seemed like he *wanted* to fight, like he was just looking for excuses. There was a big football game on and he went to a bar. It was like a perfect storm. He was drunk. He was on edge. And crowds, loud noises—since he had come home, those always set him off."

Nick sat back down on the bed, but on the end, not next to his mom. Did he really want to hear this?

"He got in an argument, they took it outside, and he ended up killing that poor man with just his bare fists and his boots. The army taught your father how to be a killer. And then it turned him loose. When he came home, he didn't remember how to be anything else."

Nick half turned to look at her.

"I had to see his wife every day at the trial." Her face was wet with tears. "This woman could have been me." She let her words trail off and swiped at her eyes. "She had two little kids, too. In another life, we could have been friends. But she . . . she hated me. My husband took her husband away from her."

"He didn't *take* him," Nick said. "He killed him."

She let out a long sigh. "You don't understand, Nick. He didn't only kill that poor man that day. Don destroyed himself, too. He blew up two families at the same time. I tried to talk to her once, but she said, 'You can still go visit your husband in prison. The only place I can talk to my husband is at the cemetery.'" Her voice shook. "Society doesn't want to see the families behind the mug shots. But we exist. I didn't ask for this to happen. But I have had to pay for this. I raised two boys alone on one salary instead of two. And I've learned not to tell people. Because if you do, they think you deserved it. That it was your fault for not knowing what he was capable of."

WHERE WERE YOU?

KYLE KNOCKED ON THE DOOR, OPENING IT before Nick even answered.

"Dude! Mom said the police questioned you about that girl!"

His brother didn't look scared. He looked excited. Maybe that was how killers reacted to scary things.

"Look, don't tell Mom," Nick said. "But they said they found DNA at the scene. There's a way they can test just a part of the male chromosome and look for a match. It matched—it matched Dad! That's how I found out about him. And the cops said it had to be a relative of his. That means it's me or you. And I know it's not me." As he said the words, their meaning sank in even deeper.

"You're joking, right?" Kyle stared at him incredulously. "You're my brother. You've known me all your life. Can you really think that?"

"I thought I knew who my dad was, and I was wrong about that."

"That's because you never knew him. You only knew this image of him you built up in your mind."

"How is that any different from you? How well do I really know you?"

"Please! Have you thought that maybe the police are just messing with you? Lying to you to get you to confess?"

"I saw the lab report."

Kyle rolled his eyes. "Or you saw what looked like a lab report. They were just trying to get you to confess. They weren't trying to get you to think it was me."

"So where were you that night, Kyle? Because I know you weren't home."

"All right." Kyle raised his eyebrows. "You want to know the truth? I was there that night."

"What?"

"I was there. At the Last Exit."

"Oh my God, you did it." It was his worst fear come to life. Not for himself, but for his brother.

"No." Kyle shook his head, sounding irritated. "No! Of course I didn't do it. I just went there because I couldn't sleep, that's all. You know Mom. She sleeps like the dead. When I couldn't, I just got up and walked down to the bar. It's not even about the beer. It's just a place I can loosen up, have fun, maybe meet some girls. Older girls."

"Uh-huh," Nick said, not knowing what was true.

"I even saw that girl. That Lucy Hayes. I watched her walk in, and about twenty seconds later she picked up two beers and dumped them on this dude and this girl. And then the bartender said he was going to call the cops. I took off even before she did. My fake ID is not that good. And I knew Mom would go ballistic if she found out I was going to a bar. I guess now you know why."

Could his brother be telling the truth? "Do you think someone else who was at the bar might have done it?"

Kyle shrugged. "I don't know. The two she dumped the beer on were pretty mad."

"Did you see anything when you were walking home?"

"Not really. It's pretty quiet that time of night." He looked up at the ceiling, remembering. "I remember a blue pickup passing me, one of those cool old Chevys from the fifties. Other than that, nothing. But I never got less than a few yards from that girl. I certainly didn't touch her. You have to believe me."

"I do," Nick said. "Of course I do."

But he didn't. Not really. Because according to the DNA, it had to be one of them who killed her. And if it wasn't his dad and it wasn't him, then it had to be Kyle.

PUSHED TO THE EDGE

"OVER HERE!" ALEXIS WAVED AT RUBY when the other girl walked into Stumptown Coffee. Nick had wanted to meet here, and Alexis had to admit it was cool, with its exposed brick and hipster vibe. But she couldn't afford to drop nearly four dollars on a latte. Instead she had gotten a house coffee. Which was still expensive.

While Alexis waited for Ruby to order, she cradled the warm mug in her hands and thought about Bran. His confession had brought them closer together, knocked down a wall she hadn't even known existed. They were getting together again tonight.

But first she had to help Nick. Or try to help him.

Carrying a drink and a pastry, Ruby made her way to the table. "Have you read the paper yet today?" she demanded as she put down her things.

Alexis shook her head. Reading the paper seemed like something only old people did.

"There's a paper in that bin by the door." Ruby took a

small foil packet from her backpack. "Go get the metro section."

Alexis followed her instructions. She started reading the story as she walked back.

POLICE SEE PROGRESS IN MURDER CASE

PORTLAND—Four days after Lucy Hayes was found stabbed in a vacant lot in Portland, police say they have identified a possible suspect in her murder.

"We have interviewed several people who could be suspects and eliminated all but one," Homicide Detective Rich Meeker said. "We're putting together a solid case against this person, including DNA evidence."

Meeker said the suspect was a male teenager, but he would not identify him further, saying he did not want to jeopardize the investigation.

A 21-year-old college student, Hayes was discovered near death Monday morning in a vacant lot in Southwest Portland. She was found a few blocks from the Last Exit Pub and Grill, which she had left the previous night on foot. She was killed by a single stab wound.

A private funeral will be held today for Hayes.

Accompanying the article was a photo of Lucy Hayes with a man, his face covered by a black dot. He had his arm around her shoulder. Both of them were dressed semiformally, like for a wedding or a dance.

Alexis felt queasy. To the general public, "male teenager" didn't say much. But if you knew that the police had taken Nick from school and questioned him for hours, it was pretty clear who they meant.

The sharp smell of rubbing alcohol made her look up. Holding her fork with a napkin, Ruby was painstakingly wiping the tines and handle with a small white wet square.

"You never know who's touched something that's kept in a communal container," she said, giving her fork one final squint-eyed inspection.

Ruby's mind worked in mysterious ways. But maybe it was good that it worked the way it did. Alexis hadn't thought anything of it yesterday when Nick texted them, half bragging about how he was consulting with the police. But Ruby's increasingly frantic texts telling him to be careful and Nick's radio silence had slowly changed her mind.

"It sounds like they're sure Nick's guilty." Alexis folded up the paper.

"You know he didn't do it, right?" Ruby looked at her for a half second and then her gaze slid away.

Alexis hesitated. She didn't want to believe Nick had done it, but was it possible? Nick was impulsive. He didn't like rules. On callouts, they were supposed to wear their SAR helmets at all times, but Nick wouldn't put on his until one of the leaders or an adult reminded him. She had also seen occasional flashes of impatience and anger. What would Nick do if he were pushed to the edge?

And he was so awkward around girls. He could barely look her in the eye—and not just because he sometimes was staring at her chest. Sometimes he was staring at his own feet. Stammering and mumbling.

But there were other facets of Nick. He could be kind, generous, even unexpectedly brave. Were those two sides of the same coin? Was he also capable of unexpected violence?

Nick wasn't perfect. But he was her friend. The same was true for Ruby. And she was sure the other two would say the same about her.

All this flashed through her mind in a few seconds. She shook her head. "No, I don't believe it. Not Nick."

"We've got to figure out a way to prove it." With nearly surgical precision, Ruby cut off a segment of her pastry.

"And how are we supposed to do that? How do you prove a negative?"

As Alexis's question hung in the air, Nick pushed open the door. His eyes were sunken, his shoulders hunched. At the counter, he spoke to the barista so softly that she had to ask him to repeat his order.

He shuffled over to their table. "Sure you guys are okay with sitting with me?" He tried on a smile.

Alexis patted the bench beside her. "Come on. Sit down."

He did as she ordered, but he didn't slide any closer.

"Why were you walking so oddly?" Ruby demanded.

Alexis tried to kick her under the table but only connected with the center post. Nick didn't need to be nitpicked when he was clearly falling apart.

He leaned back and looked at his feet. "Remember how they sent me home in shower shoes? The cops took some of my clothes at my house and all my shoes. These belong to my brother. He's got bigger feet." When he lifted his head, he caught sight of the newspaper. "And with what the cops are telling the media, they might as well have drawn a big target on my back. Harriman was all chatty with the school secretary yesterday. She likes to talk. Half the kids at school probably know now." He scrubbed his face with his hands. "I might as well give up right now. The cops aren't ever going to take any other answer than me having done it."

Alexis thought of something. "You throw up at the sight of blood. But we didn't find any vomit at the scene."

Nick rubbed his temple. "I'm pretty sure they won't think that's proof."

"That's why we need to figure out who really did it," Ruby said. "Because the cops won't. Or can't." She made a humming noise. "It's likely they found some of her DNA on your things, and that could be making them more suspicious. After all, you crawled through her blood on Monday."

"Harriman knew I got her blood on my gloves," Nick objected.

"There could still have been a transfer from your gloves to something else that's making them more suspicious." Ruby speared the last bite of her pastry.

"And there's my dad being a killer," Nick said.

Alexis blinked. "What?"

She sat stunned while Nick told her the truth about his father. How many times had Nick boasted about him or talked about how he planned to follow in his footsteps? She couldn't imagine how he was feeling now. Or maybe she could, at least a little. Her mom was mess, too. Her mom was *her* shameful secret. But at least she had grown used to it.

Nick finished by saying, "And the cops said they found my DNA on Lucy's hand."

"That's not what they said," Ruby corrected him. "If it was a full profile, then yeah, DNA is as unique as a fingerprint and they could say it was you and no one else. But what they're talking about is just a few places on the Y chromosome. Did that report say what the chances were that another person would also match what they found?"

"There were so many numbers." Nick looked up, remembering. "I think it was one in 244."

"That's all? I wonder if that means 244 men, since they were just looking at the Y chromosome, or 244 people. Either way, that still adds up to a lot of other people who could have left it. There's probably more than 244 people walking down this street right now." All three of them turned to look out the window. "I did some reading last night, and a lot of times a Y-STR would yield a much smaller pool, like only one in a thousand." Ruby smiled. "One of your ancestors must have had a lot of kids. And since we know you never touched that Lucy girl, the little piece of DNA they found has to belong to some distant relative of yours."

Instead of looking reassured, Nick pressed his hand to his mouth. He spoke so softly that they both had to lean forward to hear him over the roar of the espresso maker. "There's something you guys don't know. That nobody knows." He stopped.

"What?" Alexis prompted.

"Kyle told me he was there. At the same bar Lucy was."

"Well, there's your explanation." Ruby was unfazed. "He must have brushed past her or something."

Nick shook his head. "Kyle said he never got that close to her."

Someone was lying, Alexis thought. But was it Harriman? Or Kyle? She took a sip of her coffee, but it was now cold and bitter.

"Then there has to be some other explanation," Ruby said.

"I don't know what to think." Nick's eyes looked shiny. "Kyle doesn't even care about knives. But it seems like it has to be me or him. And I know it's not me. So it has to be him."

"The Unibomber's brother recognized his brother's writing style when they printed his manifesto in the paper," Ruby said. "Ultimately he went to the police. Even knowing that his brother would go to prison and might even be sentenced to death."

Nick looked miserable. "If I did that, it would kill my mom."

As far as Alexis was concerned, their priority was saving Nick. If his brother had done it, then that was terrible, but it was far worse to think of Nick going to prison for something he hadn't done. An idea occurred to her. She opened the paper and looked at the photo of the dead girl again. Nick shifted on the hard bench and looked away. "How much do you weigh, Ruby?" she asked.

Any other girl might have hesitated. Ruby just said, "One hundred twelve point four."

"Point four?" Alexis echoed.

"My mom has a Weight Watchers scale. It weighs in increments of one-tenth of a pound."

"And how much do you weigh, Nick?"

Nick was the one who hesitated, clearly trying to figure out what the "right" answer was. "Hundred sixty." Sitting taller, he squared his shoulders.

Alexis narrowed her eyes. "Really?"

"Um, maybe a little less."

"Look at this picture of Lucy. She's about the same height as the guy standing next to her. I would guess she weighed at least what Ruby does."

"So?"

"Let's go back to the field. Go back and see if you can drag Ruby as far as they said the killer did."

"What?" Nick gritted his teeth. "You don't think I'm that strong?"

"Don't get huffy. Have you ever had to drag someone who's deadweight? I have, and it's hard." Even though Alexis weighed more than her bone-thin mom, it was almost impossible to move her if she was not responsive. "I just don't think you could have done what they're saying." She didn't say anything about Kyle. She had seen him at the crime scene, and he was clearly bigger than Nick.

They bused their table and then went out to Ruby's car. A minute later Ruby looked in her rearview mirror. "That's weird."

Nick twitched. "What?"

"I think someone's following us."

Suddenly she was turning right, hard enough that they all swayed in their seats. At the end of the block, she turned right again, her eyes darting back and forth between her rearview mirror and the road ahead. She repeated the same move two more times. Alexis realized they had just driven in a big square.

Ruby settled back, satisfied. "Well, I either lost them or they were never following us in the first place."

FIX THIS THING

KENNY READ THE WORDS A FIFTH TIME. *"We're putting together a solid case against this person, including DNA evidence."* Meeker said the suspect was a male teenager, but he would not identify him further, saying he did not want to jeopardize the investigation.

A teenage boy, one whose DNA had been found on the dead girl. Kenny had no idea who it was or how it had happened. All he knew was that he himself was twenty years past being a teenager. And he had worn gloves that night.

The tight strings inside him loosened. The police knew nothing. Better than that, what they thought they knew was wrong.

Picking up his cup of coffee, Kenny went into the living room. He looked through a crack in the blinds at the vacant lot across the street. For years, he had ignored it, or tried to, while his mother complained it was bringing down their property value. Sometimes teenagers would hang out on the back side, smoking cigarettes or even marijuana. And during the summers, little kids would occasionally pick the blackberries from the thorny bushes, their faces smeared with purple juice. But mostly the lot was ignored.

Now no one could ignore it.

He stiffened. Across the street, three teenagers—two girls and a boy—were getting out of a car.

What were they doing? He pressed closer, his breath fogging the glass. He recognized them from Monday. Kids from Search and Rescue. Kenny had even eavesdropped on the boy and his brother.

The three teenagers were talking, pointing, gesturing. And then they moved deeper into the lot until they were next to the blackberry bushes. The spot where it had happened. The redheaded girl lay down on her back. The boy reached down, grabbed her under the arms, and began to drag her.

Back to the spot where *Kenny* had left her. Left her in a blind panic.

But now he felt coldly rational.

He needed to fix this thing. This mistake he had made. But how?

The kid was struggling. He was nearly bent in half, but he'd managed to haul the redheaded girl only a few feet.

The blond girl pushed him aside and tried to do it herself. She actually seemed to be stronger than the dark-skinned boy.

All three of them froze at a sudden sound. So did Kenny. Cop cars. Three cars sliding in from three directions.

And then the cops were out and running. The red-haired girl got to her feet. The black boy slowly raised his hands. One cop—Kenny recognized him as Rich Meeker, the one who had stopped by to ask what Kenny had seen—was holding out something small. Smaller than a toothbrush. And Kenny realized what it was.

And how he could fix everything.

NOT LIKE I'M GOING ANYWHERE

IN THE DISTANCE, A SIREN WAILED. IT WAS joined by a second. And a third. All of them getting louder. It reminded Nick of Monday—had that not even been a week ago?—of how the sirens had screamed past his house to converge on the spot where Lucy's body had been found.

The same place they were now.

Ruby rolled to her feet, her fox-like face alert. Alexis looked down the street and then turned to stare at Nick with wide eyes.

Understanding dawned just as the cop cars—one unmarked and two black-and-whites—raced up to the lot. Meeker's car had barely come to a stop before he was out the door.

"Nick Walker," he called out, "I have a warrant for your DNA." The two other cops were behind him at an angle, as if preparing for Nick to make a run for it.

Even if he were that stupid, where was he going to go? Nick had no friends in other cities. He had no car. He had no passport. He had twelve dollars in his wallet. And no credit cards.

So Nick walked forward with his hands up. And then he opened his mouth.

Two hours later Nick was in his room, lying on his bed with his arm across his eyes. He kept replaying how the cops had looked at him. How Meeker had snarled, "So you decided it was a good idea to act it out—on the day of her funeral? I knew you were sick, boy, but that is stone-cold."

His cell phone rang. He didn't bother to move.

For one thing, who would be calling him? All his friends texted. His mom called sometimes, but not from the living room, which was where she was right now. He had told her about the DNA test. She was sure it would clear him.

He wasn't so sure.

His phone rang again, but Nick stayed stuck in a loop of anxiety.

What was going to happen next? He knew he hadn't touched that girl. So he shouldn't be worried about what the DNA test would show. But would the fact that his DNA didn't match be enough to convince the cops he hadn't done it? They certainly had seemed convinced earlier. And they had asked if he had an accomplice. So even if the DNA didn't match, they still might not rule him out.

His phone rang a third time.

And even if they decided to move on, they surely wouldn't move very far. Instead, they would look closer at Kyle, who had admitted to Nick that he had seen Lucy that night. Was there some way Kyle could have touched her coat?

Or even killed her?

Either way, Nick was sure something terrible was going to happen. The noose was tightening around their family, and it was going to catch one of them.

On the fourth ring, he rolled over. And saw OREGON STATE CORRECTIONAL FACILITY on the caller ID. He pressed the button.

"Hello?"

A woman said in a clipped tone, "Will you accept a collect call from Eldon Walker?"

Would he? Should he? The man who had ruined all their lives? The man who had killed some poor guy just because he had been in the wrong place at the wrong time? The man whose blood ran in Nick's veins, who had given him half his DNA?

"Yes," he heard himself saying.

"Is this Nick?" A deep rumbling voice. Did he recognize it? It was like getting a call from a ghost.

"Yeah," he managed. He put his hand on his chest, willing his heart to slow down.

"This is your dad. Your mom told me you know the truth now."

"Mom?" Glancing at his door, he lowered his voice. "You mean she talks to you?" The way his mom had spoken about his dad, it had sounded like she had cut all ties.

His dad made a sound that wasn't quite a chuckle. "Not regularly, no. She does let me know how you kids are doing. And she told me about this mix-up about the DNA.

About how the police are questioning you. I think she blames me for that."

"Well, *Dad*," Nick gave the word a sarcastic spin, "I guess if you hadn't *killed* someone, they wouldn't have your DNA to match me to. And they wouldn't be thinking I might be the killer type."

A sigh echoed down the line. "I know you're angry, Nick, and I guess you have every right to be. But it would mean a lot to me if you would come down tomorrow and talk to me."

"What do you mean? You mean, like, visit you in prison?"

"Of course in prison. It's not like I'm going anywhere."

Nick stalled for time. "I don't even know how I would get there. For sure Kyle's not going to loan me his car."

"I've already talked about this with your mom. She'll drive you."

Anger flashed through him. He was tired of people making decisions for him. "So you guys have already decided on this without even talking to me first?"

"She said it's your call. That she would take you if you agreed."

"Whatever you want to talk about—why can't you just talk about it now? On the phone?"

"Because I want to see you, Nick. Is that asking so much, for your old man to see you for the first time in twelve years?"

THE SOLDIER
OR THE KILLER

"THIS WAY," THE DEPUTY SAID TO NICK. THEY went through a series of doors, each one closing with a solid *thunk*. Nick didn't see anyone besides the deputy, but the cameras mounted in the corners let him know that he was being seen. He breathed shallowly, trying to ignore the stink of sweat, sewage, and disinfectant.

Was this a foretaste of what awaited him? Surrounded by metal detectors and men with guns, by electronic doors and bad smells? No wonder his mom had said she didn't want to go in.

When the deputy opened the last door, they were facing a wall that held a row of Plexiglas windows separated by chest-high cinder block partitions. Each cheerless cubicle held a single battered wooden chair.

The deputy pointed at the first one and left. Nick was too nervous to sit. Instead, he ran his fingertips over the scratched and scarred counter that jutted out from under the window. It felt like some kind of reverse Braille. How many people had been here before him? Their desperation and depression still hung in the stale air. The ghosts of palm prints marked the Plexiglas, showing where prisoners and visitors had come as close to touching as they could.

He started back when a man, accompanied by a guard, walked into the room on the other side of the glass. He wore jeans and a denim shirt over a navy-blue T-shirt. On his feet were the same kind of shower shoes Nick had been given at the police station. Yesterday, Nick's mom had taken him to the mall and bought him a pair of shoes so he wouldn't have to keep wearing Kyle's.

Nick's heart felt like it was going to beat out of his chest. Of all the ways he had imagined his father, it had never been like this. This man was a stranger. The dad in his photos was way younger than this guy, with his hair cut almost to the scalp and flecked with gray. His eyes were set deep in a dark, shiny face full of creases. A mustache bracketed his full lips.

Even though his mom had talked about their faces having the same shape, Nick could see no way in which they were alike. His hands curled into fists so tight that his fingernails cut into his palms.

Staring at him through the Plexiglas, his dad slowly lowered himself into a chair, his eyes never leaving Nick's. The deputy stepped out of sight.

His dad picked up the black corded phone from the wall and motioned for Nick to do the same.

After a pause, he sat down. He uncurled his fist and picked up the heavy black phone, trying not to think about how many hands had handled it, how many lips had rested against the mouthpiece.

"Look at you." His dad blinked rapidly. His eyes were

shiny. "The last time I saw you, you were four. I mean, I've seen pictures, of course, but it's not the same. How tall are you now?"

It took Nick a second to answer. There was a keloid scar across the back of his dad's left hand, just above the knuckles. It looked like it had come from fighting. Maybe it had happened the night he killed that guy, ruined so many lives besides his own.

"Five ten," Nick finally said, adding an inch. Maybe an inch and a half. He couldn't believe they were talking about something as stupid as how tall he was. "They let me think you were dead."

His dad's voice sharpened. "Your mom made a good decision. Don't you second-guess her." He shook his head and looked away. "Besides, is it that much of a lie? The old Don Walker *is* dead."

Nick wondered which Don he meant. The soldier or the killer? He wished he were anywhere but here. He felt drained. Dull and heavy. What a waste. His dad had taken that guy's life and ruined his own, and for what? For what?

"I used to brag about you at school." The back of his neck heated up as he remembered. "I used to google your name, but I didn't realize it was just a nickname." So many things he hadn't known.

"Your mom says you want to go into the army like I did. I'm here to talk some sense into you."

"*You're* here? Don't you mean I'm here?"

His dad straightened up in his chair. "Don't you talk to me like that. I'm still your father."

Nick snorted. "How can you say that? You were never there for us."

"I wanted to be. Don't you think I wanted to be?" His eyes burned into Nick.

"Yeah, well you couldn't. Because you threw your life away."

"Exactly. Do you think I want that for you?" His jaw tightened. "I was the same way when I was your age. Thinking I knew everything. Thinking I knew what I was doing when I joined up. That's why your mom wanted me to try to talk some sense into you. See, what kind of rational human being is going to sign up to go out and kill other human beings? They don't talk about that part very much, do they? No, it's all about travel and adventure and teamwork. And being a man." Flecks of spittle were landing on the Plexiglas. "They don't talk about what it's like to watch an IED blow up the Humvee in front of you, see your friend with his legs gone, hold him when he dies. They don't tell you about any of that."

Nick was silent.

"So instead they try to tell you you'll be part of something special, that you'll learn all these great skills, that Uncle Sam will take care of you. It's all bull. The army builds you up. They tell you that you're larger than life. That you're like a superhero. And if you feel you're anything less, well then that just means you're weak-minded."

Listening to his dad, Nick couldn't believe he was here, as if he had stepped into one of those bad Lifetime movies his old babysitter had liked to watch. Women who found out their husbands had a whole other family in a different state, girlfriends who found out their boyfriend was really a serial killer. He would fit right in. A son who found out his dad wasn't really dead.

"When you leave the army, you're still not gone," his dad said. "You're still reacting to it, even when you're home—what happened back there controls your thoughts, your dreams. Your nightmares. You're too young to remember this, but I came back afraid to drive. Afraid to talk to people I'd known my whole life. I was so afraid of crowds that I had trouble going to the grocery store or the mall. I couldn't take you kids to the zoo. A stranger would smile at me and my heart would speed up because I'd think they must be planning to attack. Every night I would patrol the house, make sure everything was locked and shut and that nobody could get in anywhere."

Nick nodded, but he wasn't even sure his dad saw him.

"One time I saw a man standing on the roof of an office building and I dove to the ground, like he was a sniper. I knew it was crazy. I was thinking, he's either a sniper or he's going to radio ahead. And then I tried to tell myself, this is Portland. There's no snipers on the roof, nobody's going to blow me up here." He shook his head, looking disgusted. "I came back a bomb, Nick. And then I blew up."

Nick realized he had been hoping his dad would offer some kind of explanation. A reason for everything that had happened. Maybe even claim mistaken identity. After all, if the cops were wrong about Nick, couldn't they have been wrong about his dad?

But it was clear his dad had done both things. Gotten a Bronze Star and killed a man with his bare fists. So what did that make his dad? Could his dad still be a hero if he was also a killer? But if Hitler had saved a baby from a fire in between ordering Jews to be carted off to death camps, he would still be just as evil as before. Wouldn't he?

"It's because of you that they think I did this thing," Nick said. "Killed this girl. Lucy—"

His dad cut him off with a slash of a hand. "Whatever you did or didn't do, Nick, I don't want to know. Don't talk about it."

"You really think I—"

His dad leaned forward, his teeth gritted. "Shut it. You think just because you're sitting in that little booth and talking through a handset that no one's paying attention? There are cameras, microphones. They're watching you right now."

But what did it matter? Nick hadn't done anything wrong. Everyone else had. His mom had lied to him, and so had Kyle. His dad had killed somebody.

"That's why you're here, Nick." His dad nodded. "They wanted me to talk to you."

"What?"

"Why do you think we're alone instead of in the general visiting room? They bent all kinds of rules to make this happen. Usually it takes sixty days to get a visitor okayed. This took one." He held up his index finger for emphasis.

"Why?" Nick was still confused.

"They wanted me to get you to confess. They promised me I could get assigned to the library if I did."

"What?" Nick felt a dawning sense of horror. "You sold me out for library duty?"

"I wanted to see you. See how you turned out. So I got that, but I'm not doing the other." He breathed in and out, the sound rough. "And I'm telling you right now, Nick. Shut up. Do not say one word to anybody, not me, not your mom, not your friends, especially not the cops. And get yourself a good lawyer."

"But I didn't do it!"

His dad continued as if he hadn't spoken. "I hear they're talking about prosecuting you as an adult. Kids your age—they don't last that long in Gen Pop. Not all in one piece, anyway. But if that happens, I'll try to protect you. I've got some juice in here."

"But you're acting like I did it. I didn't. You have to believe me."

His dad slapped his hand on the counter. "I already told you. Don't talk about it. Don't say one word." His face was closed down, like someone had pulled down the blinds in his eyes. They were pure black, with no pupil visible. "Just know that I love you, Son."

The deputy came into the room, his hand on the butt of his gun. "Okay, Walker, this little show is over." When his dad didn't move, he grabbed him by the arm and dragged him backward.

CROSSES OVER THEIR EYES

S UNDAY STARTED THE WAY MOST OF RUBY'S days did. Before she even got out of bed, she clicked through the crime stories on local news sites. BOUNCER ACQUITTED IN SHOOTING. $10,000 REWARD OFFERED FOR IDENTITY OF HIT-AND-RUN DRIVER. SUSPECT ARRESTED IN ARSON AT NIGHT CLUB. Nothing too exciting.

And nothing more about Lucy Hayes. Just the same information the paper had had, with the police claiming that they were building a case against a single teenaged male suspect.

After breakfast, her phone buzzed with a text.

911 Assist Clack Co—Elderly mushroom picker—
Meet @ 1000

After she texted back that she could come, Ruby texted Nick. Want me to pick you up?

Can't go. On my way to visit my dad.

Ruby blinked. Then she texted back. In prison?

Yes.

She wasn't sure how to respond. What would a supportive friend do? This particular set of circumstances hadn't been covered in any movie or book she was familiar with. While a drawled "Wow!" accompanied by a smile seemed to be an acceptable verbal response to almost anything, (a) Nick couldn't see her expression, and (b) "Wow" didn't seem quite right. She finally settled on "Good luck." Without even a smiley face. Then she went out to tell her parents that the team was being called out.

In the sheriff's van, she and Alexis sat next to each other. It was the first time they had been on a callout together without Nick.

"Where is your triple musketeer?" Dimitri asked as he clambered on behind them.

She and Alexis exchanged a look. "Nick couldn't make it out today," Alexis finally said.

When they were under way, they spoke in low whispers that blended in with the rumble of the van's motor.

"I'm worried about Nick," Ruby said.

"The DNA's not going to match," Alexis said confidently. "It can't."

But Alexis's reaction was emotional, not logical. Ruby had tried to analyze it objectively. Certain factors were associated with teens who became killers. She was pretty certain Nick's home life was stable. He wasn't suicidal or depressed. As far as she could tell, he didn't use drugs or alcohol. He wasn't a member of a gang or a cult—unless, she thought with a faint smile—SAR counted as one. He wasn't mentally ill.

Was he bullied at school? That she was a little less certain about.

The one thing that gave her pause was that he liked violence. She had heard him with some of the other guys in SAR talking about playing first-person shooter video games. Although if he was talking about them with other guys in SAR, then that made Nick no better or worse than them, right?

Ruby had also seen his drawings. Everyone who had happened to sit by him had probably noticed them. On the edge of every handout or piece of notebook paper he doodled dinosaurs, arrows, hatchets, people with guns shooting at other people with guns, people bleeding, people with crosses over their eyes she assumed were meant to be dead. Sometimes he drew some guy who looked even more like a cartoon than the others, with swollen-looking arms. Even though Nick had never said, Ruby thought this guy was supposed to be Nick. Nick in some alternate universe where he wasn't skinny with his hair hanging in his eyes.

But in Nick's drawings, the buff guy was the good one. Fighting off the bad guys and saving pretty girls.

Not knifing pretty girls and leaving them in some vacant lot to die.

"He does like knives a lot," she ventured to Alexis. How many times had she seen him playing with a knife, showing it off, trying to fling it into a tree trunk (and missing every time). It might be possible to construct a set of circumstances in which he had accidentally killed that girl.

"So?" Alexis said. "Every person in this van has a knife, even if it's just a Leatherman tool." She pressed her lips together. "And there's no way he could have bashed that girl's head in with a brick. You saw what he was like just getting some of her blood on his gloves."

Ruby wasn't sure this was convincing. "The cops would probably just say that was his guilty conscience."

A half hour later Jon parked the van in a forested area next to two others, as well as a pickup truck. A little farther down the road sat an old blue Ford Taurus.

Chris, the sheriff's deputy, briefed them. "The point last seen is that vehicle." He pointed at the Taurus. "Yesterday a hiker came across an older woman mushroom hunting near it. She said it was just for the day. She was dressed fairly warmly, but all he remembers her carrying are a bag and a walking stick. This morning the hiker was returning when he noticed the vehicle was still here. It was unlocked and there was no sign of the owner. So he alerted the sheriff's department."

Chris looked down at his notes. "The car's owner is a seventy-seven-year-old woman named Lottie Landsman. She's about five eight and one-eighty. The hiker says she was wearing black pants and a purple hooded jacket. Her son says she knows the woods well. Then again, she is seventy-seven years old and has a bad knee. She's on a handful of medications for blood pressure, cholesterol, and acid reflux, but she could go at least another twenty-four hours before she would feel any side effects. Her son says she's very independent. And maybe getting to be a little forgetful. Daylight saving time only ended a few weeks ago, and she may not have factored that in."

Jon added, "Mushroom pickers can get so focused on looking for mushrooms that they tend to wander. When they decide they're done, they look up and realize they don't recognize anything, and they often have no idea which direction they came from. Mushroom pickers are hard to track, since they aren't going 'to'"—he made air quotes—"any specific place at all. They're just looking for mushrooms."

"It's imperative that we find her today," Chris continued. "Due to her age and the weather, the possibility she could survive a second night is slim. There's a tracking dog already out. But so far she hasn't turned up anything definitive. Hasty teams have cleared the local trails. And we have containment running the roads." He paused. "But no sign of her. So far, all we really know is where she isn't. That's where you guys come in. We're going to do a grid search today. First, we need to figure out critical separation."

In class, they had learned that to cover the most ground in a grid search, the searchers needed to be as far apart as possible and still see the smallest object they were looking for. A person was fairly big, so they could be pretty far apart, but not so far that the team members couldn't see each other.

Chris shrugged off his pack and put it down. "Imagine that this is an unresponsive person." Each team member took a slightly different angle and walked away to the point where they could still see the pack and identify it. Then they all counted their paces from that point back to the pack and called out the number.

Mitchell averaged the results—in his head, which impressed Ruby—and used that number of paces to decide that the critical spacing was thirty feet. That way, if Lottie was lying unconscious between two searchers, she would still be seen. Critical spacing was affected not only by the size of the object, but also by the terrain, the weather, and more.

Because the line would otherwise be too spread out, he split them into two groups. Each would use one side of the road as a guide. "Remember to look up, down, and all around," Mitchell said as they set their lines and got ready to count off.

Ruby looked under every bush and tree, while at the same time trying not to twist an ankle on a root or trip on a rock. All while keeping an eye on Ezra, who was on her left. They had done practice search grids before, but those had been in a fairly open area. Rugged terrain and dense brush made staying in line and on track a challenge. Every few minutes they would blow their whistles and listen for a yell. But each time, there was only silence.

After about an hour, Mitchell's radio crackled and he called a halt. When everyone had gathered around, he said, "We just heard from the dog handler."

"So they found her?" Max asked. People were already starting to relax, rolling their necks, reaching for snacks.

"No." Mitchell screwed up his face. "It turns out the dog was following the scent of the hiker who called it in. Not the mushroom picker. Nobody told the dog handler that someone else had been in the car, so she used the driver's seat as the scent article. The hiker sat there and looked through the glove compartment to get Lottie's name before he called us. So his scent was not only fresher than Lottie's, but he was also probably putting out more adrenaline."

It was so frustrating, Ruby thought as they lined back up and began to search again. The dog had been following a promising clue, but it hadn't meant anything.

Something about the idea teased her. Something that might apply to Nick. But the harder she tried to pin it down, the more it slid away.

And then she forgot all about it when, after blowing their whistles for the millionth time, they heard a faint cry from the bottom of a steep embankment.

"Help! I've broken my ankle!"

CHAPTER 42
NICK
MONDAY

YOU'RE THE ONE

ON MONDAY, NICK HADN'T EVEN MADE IT through the main doors of the school when Carson Canterbery detached himself from a group of guys and marched straight up to him. Carson was a senior and had never paid any attention to Nick before.

"So is it true?" he demanded. He leaned down so his face was just a few inches from Nick's.

"Is what true?" Nick said, stalling for time.

"There are rumors going around that you're the one who knifed that girl to death last week." Carson's breath smelled like bitter coffee.

"Of course it's not true." Nick attempted to go around, but Carson slid sideways and blocked his path. He played basketball and had six inches on Nick, easy.

"But you live right next to where she was found."

"No, it's like six blocks away. And besides, I'm not the one who did it." How did anyone know he was a suspect? From reading the paper? From Mrs. Weissig? From the police themselves?

Carson nodded rapidly, as if Nick had just confirmed everything he had heard. After giving him one last long look, he finally stepped aside.

It pretty much went like that for the rest of the day. Kids stared at him, whispered, pointed. Fell silent if he got too close. Even stepped back from him as he walked down the hall.

At lunch, the same invisible force field kept people away. Only Sasha Madigan dared to breach it. Any other day, Nick would have loved to have Sasha lean in close. But not when she did it just so she could say, "Are you really a murder suspect?"

He was silent for a long moment, holding her gaze. "You know me, Sasha. What do you think?"

"Uh, I don't think you did it." But she was backing away when she said it.

When the classroom phone rang in his art class an hour later, Nick wasn't surprised to be told he was wanted down at the office. Everyone, even the teacher, was silent as he gathered up his things. Some people looked away, not meeting his eyes. Others looked at him as if he weren't a person but a particularly fascinating traffic accident that had happened on the other side of the free-way. Nick resolved never to look at anyone like that ever again. Those people had probably never thought that some-day someone might be staring at them as if they were a different species. As if they were a photo printed on paper, not a real person.

When he walked into the office, Mrs. Weissig stiffened. Her jaw jutted forward, making her look like a toad. But she wouldn't look him in the eye, just told him that Mr. Loughlin was waiting for him.

The principal steepled his fingers. "Look, Nick, we've been hearing from parents. They don't feel comfortable having you in school right now."

Nick didn't hurry to volunteer anything. He wasn't going to make this easy for anyone. Not when it was his life that was being trashed. "And why is that?"

"The thing is, Nick, we've been informed that you're a person of interest in an ongoing murder investigation."

Nick looked the principal straight in the eyes, kept looking even when the older man looked away. "You really think I'm a murderer?"

"Of course not, Nick." He managed to look Nick in the face again. "It's just that we have to look at the needs of all the students." *Nick, Nick, Nick.* The principal was using his name as often as a used-car salesman, and he was just as convincing. "This situation—which we all hope is only temporary—isn't conducive to a learning environment. Not for you, Nick, and not for the other students."

"So you're just going to throw me under the bus?"

"Of course not. This is just a temporary situation."

"Uh-huh." He didn't bother to hide his sarcasm.

"Look, Nick, this isn't about just you. It's about the entire school. I have to think about the other eight hundred kids. What's the most fair thing for everyone? If you're innocent, you have nothing to worry about. We'll provide you with a tutor until this thing gets straightened out." He got to his feet. "Let me walk you out."

This couldn't be happening to him. A week ago he had saved a little girl's life. Now everyone thought he was a killer, not a hero.

Mr. Loughlin stood at the door, waiting for him. Nick didn't know what to do. So he pushed himself to his feet and grabbed his pack.

The bell rang as they were walking out of the office. The hall was full, but people slowed down and even stopped when they saw Nick walking with Mr. Loughlin. He started when he felt the principal's hand under his elbow.

"Just to be clear," Mr. Loughlin said when they reached the city bus stop, "we don't want to see you on school grounds again." After a moment, he added, "Not until this thing is straightened out."

Nick was pretty sure that neither one of them believed that this would actually happen.

Once he got onto the bus, he turned his face toward the window and put his hand up to cover it. He closed his eyes. If anyone was staring at him, he did not want to see. As he walked home from the bus stop, Nick heard a car behind him. But it didn't pass. He looked over his shoulder. It was a brown Crown Victoria with a spotlight mounted above the driver's side mirror. An unmarked police car, but the driver, an impassive guy staring at him through sunglasses, obviously didn't care that Nick had just identified him. Nick looked closer. It was that Rich guy, Harriman's partner. And he just kept driving at the same speed as Nick walked.

As he turned onto his block, his phone rang. The caller

ID showed PORTLAND COUNTY SHERIFF. Nick didn't want to hear what they had to say. Still, his thumb pushed the green button.

"Hello?"

"Is this Nick?"

"Yeah."

"Nick, this is Deputy Nagle."

You mean Chris? Nick thought. He guessed that the days of Chris Nagle being Chris were over. "Yeah?"

"I've been having some conversations with the Portland police. For the time being, I'm taking you off the roster for Search and Rescue callouts. And we'll figure out a way for you to make up any missed classes."

Nick was silent.

"I'm sorry, but there's nothing I can do. Not until this thing is resolved." Chris didn't even bother to explain what "this thing" was.

For an answer, Nick hung up.

His dreams were all gone, stolen from him. His life was ruined. No school. No SAR. And, of course, there was no longer any point of thinking of the army.

Nearly everyone thought he was a murderer. Especially the cops. The only people who didn't were Alexis and Ruby.

He was trapped without any way out.

Except maybe there was always a way. If you were desperate enough.

After he let himself inside the empty house, he went down to the basement. He sifted through the junk drawer, through the bent screwdrivers and little screws that might come in handy, until he found the box cutter. He undid it, took out the razor blade and hid it under the insole of his shoe.

If they arrested him, he could always kill himself.

Kill himself before he ended up sharing a cell with his dad.

READY TO THROW IN THE TOWEL

KYLE CAME INTO NICK'S ROOM WITHOUT knocking.

"I don't believe it," he said, looking disgusted. "I thought I smelled cigarette smoke."

Nick took another drag on his cigarette. He had found the hidden pack when he was looking for the box cutter. He hadn't been able to find a lighter, so he had used one of the wooden kitchen matches they kept for when the gas stove was acting up.

"So these aren't yours?" He turned and blew a stream of smoke out the open window. His room was about the same temperature as outside, so he was still wearing his coat. "I found them in the basement."

"They're Mom's. She smokes about one a year when she's really stressed out." One more secret Nick hadn't been privy to. "Why in the heck are *you* smoking?"

"Why shouldn't I be?" Nick sucked in another lungful of pollutants. "I got told I wasn't welcome at both school *and* SAR today. Might as well act like the bad guy everyone thinks I am." Besides, wasn't this what people did in prison—smoked, bummed smokes, bartered with them?

"Why did they do that?"

"The cops told SAR and the school that I was a 'person of interest' in a murder case. Everyone knows what that means."

"So now you're ready to throw in the towel?" Kyle gave his head a shake. "Once they get your DNA test back, they're going to know it wasn't you. Didn't they tell you that there were other people who could match?"

"Yeah. Like you." Nick took another drag, suppressing the urge to cough. One thing about the cigarette was that it somehow allowed him to keep his face impassive, his gaze steady on Kyle.

"You don't really think that, do you?" When Nick didn't answer and didn't look away, Kyle swore, kicking one of the legs of the bed. "I already told you where I was that night. And that I never even talked to that Lucy person, let alone laid a hand on her. There's got to be some other explanation. Like some fourth cousin three times removed we don't even know about."

Did Kyle really believe that? Because Nick didn't. He just shrugged.

"What is wrong with you, man?" Kyle screwed his face up. "You were so eager to believe Dad was some big hero. And now you want to believe that I'm a killer. When neither one of those things is true." Kyle left, slamming the door behind him. Because of the open window, it shook the house.

As Nick was taking another drag, the doorbell rang,

startling him. Nobody ever rang the doorbell. He stilled, straining to hear.

"Kyle Walker?" he heard a man say. Nick didn't recognize his voice, but whoever it was definitely sounded like a cop.

"Yes?" Kyle's voice shook. So much for his certainty.

"We'd like to talk to your brother, Nick."

Without thinking, Nick took three steps toward the window, lay down on the sill, and rolled out.

He landed with a thud on his belly in the backyard. The impact knocked the air from his lungs and the cigarette from his hands.

Their yard was bordered on both sides by overgrown laurel hedges. At the back was a cinder block wall that separated their yard from Mrs. Watkins's. Even with no breath in him, he scuttled toward it, keeping low.

How many times had he crawled through this backyard, pretending to be a soldier? Now all that bear crawling, pretending he was sneaking up on the enemy, served him in good stead.

Because today he was fighting for real. Fighting for his life. He scrabbled across the yard. Through a gap at the root level of the laurels, he saw two cop cars on his street.

How long did he have? Would Kyle even try to stall them?

He was up and over the wall in a second. When he landed on the other side, he saw Mrs. Watkins's back through the window. She was drinking a cup of tea and watching TV. She didn't turn around.

Nick made it through two more yards, keeping low and moving fast. He was just lucky everyone was still at work. But the next barrier between backyards was a seven-foot-tall wooden fence. Even if he could figure out how to scale it, it felt like it would leave him too exposed.

Where was he? On his mental map, Nick thought he might be at the point where the street started to curve. He cut through the side yard and out into the front yard, sticking close to the house. He risked one glance down the street, just one.

Another cop car was skidding to a stop in front of his house. *No, no, no.*

He cut through three more front yards, darted across a busy street, and then risked a flat-out run, even though it would draw attention to him. Predators—including human beings—were hardwired to respond to sudden movement. But this wasn't a case where playing dead would do him any good. His heart felt like it would beat out of his chest. His breath was coming in gasps.

Traffic was thickening around him. The middle school up the street was letting out and parents were coming by to pick up their kids. At first, he started to cut away. But then he realized what the students were. Protective coloration. Forcing himself to slow to a walk, Nick plunged into the crowd of kids spilling out the double doors. Out of the corner of his eye, he saw a few kids glance at him curiously.

Pretending to look at his phone, he got on one of the buses. It was half full. He started walking down the aisle.

"Hey, wait a minute!" It was the bus driver, a plump balding man. "You in the blue jacket!"

Nick turned. Already new kids were climbing onto the bus. He was trapped. There was no way he could push past them and run out the door, not without the driver grabbing him. Could he run the length of the bus and somehow unlatch the emergency exit in the back before he was caught?

"Yeah?"

"You sure you're on the right bus, kid?"

He forced himself to speak calmly. "This is number twenty-one, right?" he asked, using the number he had seen on the front of the bus.

"Yes, twenty-one, that's right." The driver nodded.

"We just moved here from Seattle. This was my first day." Nick had never thought he'd be happy about being the same size as an eighth grader, but for once it was coming in handy.

"And you know your stop?"

What was he going to say when the guy asked him which one it was? He had no idea where this bus was actually going. Nick nodded, not trusting himself to speak.

"Okay, then. Welcome to Portland."

He mumbled a thank you and then took an empty seat in the middle of the bus. Keeping his head down, he sat in an aisle seat. If he didn't make eye contact, maybe no one would challenge him or ask questions. Because he was fresh out of answers.

He fished his phone from his pocket and texted Ruby.

The cops came to arrest me and I ran.

The answer came a second later.

Where are you?

He had a fresh appreciation for Ruby. Unlike everyone

else, she wasn't giving him a lecture about how he was making a terrible mistake or about how he should just turn himself in and trust that the justice system would sort everything out.

Robert Gray on bus. Pretending I'm a new student.

Turn off your phone in case they're tracking you. Get off somewhere in the middle, not at the last stop. Start to walk away fast before anyone can ask questions. Turn your phone on long enough to text me where you are, and I'll pick you up.

Thank you.

Nick pressed the button and watched the display dwindle away to nothing.

Just like the chances that he would be able to stay free.

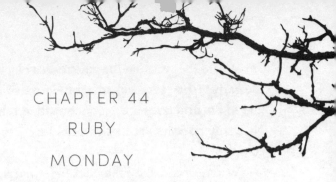

KEEP YOUR HEAD DOWN

RUBY MADE A QUICK STOP AT HOME, thankful that both her parents worked during the day, and raided her dad's closet. Before she went inside, Ruby texted Alexis.

> The cops want to arrest Nick. He's safe, for now. But we need to figure out how to prove they're wrong.

After she pulled out of her driveway, she kept an eye on her rearview mirror. That big black SUV. Was it following her? If it was the cops and they put on the siren, there was no way she could outrun them. But if they were hoping she would lead them to Nick, they might hang back and let her go. She had to lose them. As she had before, she took four right turns, one after another. Then she got on the freeway, moved rapidly to the left, and then a second later cut over two lanes to take the first exit without signaling. Finally satisfied no one was following her—if they had ever been—she started working her way in the general direction of Robert Gray Middle School.

While she was driving, she took a black ball cap from the garbage bag and tucked her hair under it. Red hair was just too distinctive. If the police realized she was helping Nick, any all-points bulletin would surely mention her hair color.

Where could she take Nick? Her parents had a cabin at the beach, but it was ninety minutes away. Just contemplating the long drive made the back of her neck itch. If the cops were looking for her car, it would be easy to spot on a lonely coastal highway. Plus what if they got to the coast and Nick needed to run again? It was a lot harder to lose yourself in a sparsely populated coastal town, especially in the off-season.

No, in town seemed best. But where?

Libraries? Too quiet.

A hotel? From her daily check of crime stories, Ruby had noticed that a couple of hotels on Barbur Boulevard frequently showed up as places where people got arrested. So it seemed likely they weren't too picky about their clientele, and they probably were happy to take cash and not ask for any ID. But most motel units only had one door, so if Nick got cornered, he wouldn't be able to escape. Besides, it was probably a bad sign that she knew the hotels as places where people were arrested. If they were on her radar, they must be on the cops' as well.

What about the airport? Thousands of people passed through it every day. If she bought Nick a suitcase to provide protective coloration, he could probably spend a couple of days there before people stopped believing he was really a traveler.

Another part of Ruby's brain was busy with a different

problem of Nick's. If the police had come to arrest him, then his DNA must have matched the DNA found on Lucy Hayes. But how was that possible? There had to be an explanation. Assuming the police hadn't made an error or planted the DNA, how could two people who didn't know each other still make contact?

Her phone buzzed. Nick had texted her the address where he was—and, she hoped, turned off his phone immediately afterward. She tapped a button to get her phone to give her directions. A minute later she spotted him, walking fast down the sidewalk, head down. He still twitched when she pulled up next to him, then scrambled into the car.

"Thank you!" He sounded out of breath. And maybe, she thought, on the verge of tears.

"Put on the cap that's in that garbage bag."

He pulled out an orange ball cap with a logo for the Oregon State Beavers. "Don't you have one with the Ducks?"

At first, Ruby thought he was serious, but when she glanced over in annoyance, he gave her a shaky grin.

"There's a coat in there, too," she said. "Trade your jacket for it." It was her dad's, just like the ball cap. They were only small changes, but they might add up to enough. If they were very lucky.

"Where are we going, anyway?" he asked as she got on Multnomah Boulevard and headed for the freeway.

"Lloyd Center Mall."

"The mall?" He let out a strangled laugh. "I don't think now is the time to go shopping."

Ruby tamped down her annoyance. "It's not just any

mall. For one thing, it's on the opposite side of the river. In Portland, people tend to stay on their side of the river. The cops will have no reason to look for you over there. You don't live on that side. You don't have friends there."

"I used to. In grade school."

"Oh." Ruby recalibrated. "Well, they probably still won't look for you there. Besides, a mall is the perfect place. Lots of other kids to blend in with. A food court, so you can eat. Restrooms, so you can go to the bathroom. A hundred stores you can pretend to be shopping at. Lots of exits. Benches to sit on. Even a movie theater. And we can get you a burner phone there."

"A burner phone?" Nick echoed. "What's that?"

"One of those cheap phones you buy for cash. The police won't know you have it, so they won't be able to track you on it. Right now they can ping your phone and if it's on, they can track you down to your exact location." Ruby felt a surge of panic. "Your phone is off, right?"

"Yeah, yeah, it is." Nick took a deep breath. "Maybe it was stupid to take off when they came to arrest me. I know I can't stay on the run forever. Or even very long. But at the same time, I'm not going to just walk up and let them put my head in the noose. I've seen those TV reports where the person is found innocent—after they've spent twenty years in prison. I don't want to not get out until I'm in my thirties. Or get killed in prison. Or never get out."

"I keep feeling like there's something I'm missing." Ruby was checking her rearview mirror every minute, but so far no one seemed to be following them. "Some explanation for how your DNA ended up on that girl's hand." That was an interesting thought. Maybe she should be thinking about something Lucy had touched. Had she been someplace Nick had been, touched something he had touched?

"The cops must have faked it."

Ruby knew she wasn't a great judge of people, but she still rebelled against the idea. "Do you really believe that? Because Harriman? I don't think he would do that." She took the exit for the mall.

"Yeah, but his partner, that Rich Meeker guy, might. He was practically spitting in my face. There was one point I thought he was going to hit me. And earlier today he was following me down the street."

In the parking lot, Ruby chose a spot in the middle, balancing the need for protective coloration with the need for isolation.

"Keep your head down," she said as they walked in. "Even if the cops put someone in the security office to watch the feed, if you don't tilt your face up they might not notice you." She walked over to a map of the mall. On the floor in front of it was a lost black glove. She picked it up and rested it on top, where it might attract more attention.

"There's a phone store on the other side." She started off, but Nick didn't follow.

"What's the matter?"

"Um, I don't have any money. Not enough for a phone, anyway."

"Don't worry. I'll cover it."

"Are you sure?"

"Of course I am. You're my friend." Even in the midst of everything, Ruby felt a warm glow saying the words.

As she and Nick walked past store after store, the lost glove stayed in her thoughts. It felt as if it were somehow connected to Lucy. It must remind her of the dead girl's lost mitten. That was it, wasn't it?

She was buying the new phone when it came to her. The guy was still counting out her change when she walked a few feet away. She barely registered his stare or Nick calling her name.

Because she knew why they had found Nick's DNA on Lucy. Found it on her even though he had never touched her.

CHAPTER 45

K

MONDAY

LAMB TO THE SLAUGHTER

"ALEXIS FROST?" KENNY SAID AS HE MOVED against the current of students streaming out the school's front door. He had gotten her name from an online article about Portland SAR, one that had helpfully included a captioned photo. On her Facebook page, she listed the name of her school. On the school's web page, he had found the time school ended.

Pretty good detective work for a guy who was supposed to be slow. How many years had he let others define him? He should have defined himself.

"Yes?" She turned toward him, holding her phone. The way she tilted her head, curious but shy, reminded him of Lucy. He felt a momentary pang, but he pushed it away.

He remembered his role. Brisk. Compartmentalized. He was modeling himself on the people who had dealt with him after his mother died. In fact, under an open winter coat, he was wearing the same suit he had worn to his mother's funeral. Because it was a suit, he figured it made him look more official.

"I'm afraid there's been an accident."

Her eyes went wide as a fawn's. Just as he had hoped, she filled in the blank so he didn't have to. "Is it my mom?"

"I'm afraid so." He nodded briskly. "She's been taken to Good Sam. They asked me to come get you." He had already turned and was walking away, as if certain she would follow. "She's been asking for you."

He heard her footsteps as she hurried to keep up with him.

Who was the smart one now? He had a girl following him, as meekly as a lamb.

Lamb to the slaughter.

COULDN'T BE HAPPENING

W HEN THE MAN TOLD ALEXIS ABOUT her mom, she was parsing Ruby's text.

The cops want to arrest Nick. He's safe, for now. But we need to figure out how to prove they're wrong.

Did that mean Nick was with Ruby? Or that she had hidden him someplace? Was it better if Alexis didn't know the answers?

As soon as she heard that her mom was in the hospital, Alexis forgot about everything else. But by the time they reached the man's old blue pickup, her footsteps were slowing down.

"What's wrong with my mom exactly?" she asked.

"I told you, she's at the hospital. Now come on, we need to get there." He stepped behind her and put a hand under her elbow. He was wearing gloves, even though his coat was unbuttoned and it was about 40 degrees.

"Tell me what happened," she demanded, turning away from him and stepping back.

"There was an accident. Your mom was driving and—"

"What?" she interrupted. "We don't even have a car."

His eyes narrowed. "Listen to me," he said, stepping toward her.

Alexis took another step back, but there was nowhere for her to go. The door handle jabbed into her lower back, and he was so close his knees crowded hers.

Instead of finishing his sentence, he jabbed something into her rib cage. Something hard. She looked down. It was a gun.

This couldn't be happening to her, could it?

"Put away your phone," he ordered.

Alexis obeyed. Mostly. But as she slid it into her purse, her thumb moved to the corner and tapped the spot that normally read "Connect." In her mind's eye, she pictured the next display and moved her thumb a quarter inch to the left. To where there should be a phone icon. She tapped again. If she had done it right, she was dialing Ruby. If she hadn't . . .

"Get in the truck and then scoot over to the driver's seat. And don't try anything, or I'll shoot you."

Alexis looked past him. They were only half a block from school, but the kids had already dispersed in all directions. No one was close enough to catch her eye.

He jabbed her again. "Do it. Or I'll kill you right now." Alexis's biology class had supplied her imagination with a neat diagram of everything that was at risk. Liver, kidneys, ovaries, duodenum. Plus some major blood vessels.

"Okay, okay," she said, opening the door and stepping up. The keys dangled from the ignition. She sat down on the bench seat and began to slide over, her eyes fixed on the other door's handle. Should she open it and run out the other side? But the man was already right next to her.

Her heart contracted. From her purse rose a tiny, tinny whisper. It was Ruby saying, "Hello, hello?"

"I'll do whatever you want." Setting her purse down in between them, she spoke louder than was necessary, trying to both cover the sound and provide Ruby a clue at the same time. "Just please don't shoot me."

"Start the truck and go straight down this street for two blocks and then turn right."

As she turned the key, Alexis caught a whiff of his rank sweat. He seemed younger and less assured than she had first thought. Maybe midthirties. About her height, but she had noticed how the suit strained against his powerful chest.

"What do you want? Why do you have a gun?" *Please don't hang up*, she mentally implored Ruby. *Figure out what's going on and get me some help.* Although wasn't it more likely that when Ruby hadn't gotten an answer she had decided it was a pocket dial and hung up? And even if Ruby could hear Alexis, what could she do?

"Don't worry about that now." He jabbed her again. "Just start driving and follow my directions."

Alexis drove past two people she vaguely knew from third period kissing on the street corner. She tried to broadcast her thoughts. *Look at me. Notice there is something wrong.*

Lost in their own world, they continued kissing. Their eyes were closed.

Following his instructions, Alexis turned right. Should she crash the truck into a telephone pole or a newspaper box, then jump out and run down the street screaming for help?

As if reading her mind, he poked the gun into her side again.

"If you try anything, I will kill you *and* anyone you ask for help."

"Okay." The word got stuck in her throat. Alexis cleared her throat and tried again. "Okay." If she acted obedient, maybe he would let down his guard.

About a half block behind them was a black car. She needed to attract attention. But subtly, so the man with the gun didn't notice. Alexis turned the wheel slightly until she was a few inches over the yellow line. With a feather-light touch, she began randomly tapping the brake. She prayed that the other driver would call 9-1-1 and report an impaired driver.

Instead, he passed her with a blaring horn and an out-thrust finger.

"Stop that!" the man said, jabbing her with the gun again. "Stop trying to attract attention. If I have to, I will kill you right *here*."

Alexis didn't like the way he phrased it. As if killing her was a given, the location the only optional part.

Think, Alexis, think! she commanded herself.

She couldn't escape him.

She couldn't rely on others for help.

So what did that leave? Maybe she could build a bridge between them. To make it so that killing her was no longer something he could think about so easily.

"Okay, okay. I'm sorry. I'll do exactly what you say."

He nodded. "Good." The pressure on the gun eased up infinitesimally. "Keep going straight."

On the off chance that Ruby was still there, she said, "I'll just keep driving on Powell. Do you want me to turn on Seventeenth?"

"No. Just go over the bridge."

"The Ross Island?" she said, although the answer was obvious. But maybe not to Ruby. If she was listening. If Alexis wasn't talking to dead air. "Where are we going, anyway?"

He put his free hand to his head. "Can't you shut up for just a second?"

"I'm just trying to understand. I mean, you must have your reasons for kidnapping me. Why are you doing this? What do you want?"

"It's not really what I want. It's just what I have to do." His lips crimped together and then he took a deep breath. "I have to kill you."

FOLLOW MY DIRECTIONS

"RUBY! RUBY!"

Nick was standing in front of her, but Ruby barely registered him. Instead, she was smoothing the outside seams of her pants with her thumbs, up and down, over and over, as her mind worked it through.

"Ruby!"

"Huh?" She blinked and forced herself to focus on him.

"What is the matter with you?" He held out her change.

She ignored it. "That glove. That glove is like the DNA. Only instead of leaving behind a glove, you left behind your DNA." In her mind's eye, she replayed how Nick had thrown up when he saw Mariana's leg, then wiped his mouth.

"What glove?" His forehead creased. "What are you talking about?"

"The one I picked up and moved." Nick still looked blank. "When we came in the mall? Like five minutes ago?" He nodded but didn't look any less confused. "If someone else came in after us and saw the glove on top of the sign, they might think that the owner set it down and forgot about it. When really I'm the one who put it there."

"Yeah, so? I don't get it."

"Remember Locard's exchange principle?" Ruby thought of how the paramedics had run to help Mariana.

"What does that have to do with anything?"

"Locard said that a criminal always leaves something at the crime scene and always takes something away." She remembered Harriman telling them that an ambulance had taken Lucy to the hospital.

"But I wasn't there. And I'm not a criminal."

Was Nick being deliberately dense? Ruby stamped her foot. "But isn't that true for *whoever* is at the scene? True for, say, the paramedics? What did they leave behind? And where did it come from? Remember how you got sick that night we helped Mariana?"

Nick grimaced. "How could I forget?"

"So some of that vomit must have gotten on her. Remember how you wiped your mouth afterward? And then you held her hand when the paramedics were working on her? Until they needed to clip on the pulse ox? They change gloves between patients, but they don't change everything. I'll bet you anything that the EMTs who took Lucy Hayes to the hospital were the same ones who helped Mariana earlier. Some of your vomit must have gotten on the pulse ox and later been transferred to Lucy."

Nick's face went slack as the implications sank in.

Just in case, Ruby spelled it out for him. "You aren't the common denominator. The paramedics are. They accidentally carried your DNA from Mariana to Lucy."

Her phone rang. Ruby was going to ignore it, but then she saw it was Alexis. Maybe she would figure it out faster than Nick had. He still looked like it was sinking in.

"Hello?" Ruby said.

No answer.

"Hello?" Ruby tried again. "Alexis?"

Nick shrugged. "She must have butt dialed you. Just hang up. We need to tell Harriman."

But Ruby heard someone talking in the background. It *sounded* like Alexis. She stuck her index finger in her other ear and closed her eyes.

"What do you want?" she heard Alexis say. "Why do you have a gun?"

And then Ruby realized there was a missing part to her equation. If Nick hadn't killed Lucy, who had? She had the sinking feeling that the answer to that question might be the person Alexis was now talking to.

A new voice spoke. "Don't worry about that now. Just start driving and follow my directions." The voice wasn't as clear as Alexis's, but it was definitely a man's.

Ruby turned, opened her eyes, and started frantically drawing on top of the counter with her index finger. The salesman looked at her like she was crazy, but Nick got it.

"Do you need a pen?"

She nodded. While Nick wrangled one, she heard more exchanges between Alexis and the man that made the hair rise on the back of her neck. When the clerk pushed the paper and pen toward her, she scribbled, "Alexis kidnapped. Can hear her talking to guy."

When Alexis started asking about turning onto Seventeenth from Powell, Ruby knew right where Alexis was. Where she and the person who was holding the gun on her were. Close to the Ross Island Bridge.

Alexis was in trouble. Did she even know whom she had dialed? Was she just hoping that whoever it was would listen, wouldn't hang up?

They needed to call the police and let them know what was happening. They couldn't use Ruby's phone without first hanging up on Alexis. And if they used Nick's phone, the cops would show up first and ask questions later. That left the new phone.

"Take notes," she wrote for Nick, and underlined it. Then she handed him the phone, pushed over the paper and pen, and tore open the package holding the new phone.

Of course, this phone didn't have Harriman's direct number, so she had to call 4-1-1. She was transferred to Central Precinct. When she asked to be transferred to Harriman, it wasn't even him who answered.

"Detective Meeker."

"I need to speak to Detective Harriman. It's urgent."

"He's busy right now. But he's my partner. What do you need?"

"Okay." The words crowded into Ruby's mouth. "Alexis Frost has been kidnapped."

"What?"

"I just got a call from Alexis. Well, maybe not from her, because she's not speaking directly to me. But I can hear her in the background talking to some guy. And she's saying things such as 'Don't shoot me.' I'm pretty sure she's with the real killer. And she was saying she was driving down Powell. Toward the Ross Island Bridge. You have to stop him before he kills her."

"Let me ask you something. Have you been drinking?"

"What?" Ruby felt her face get hot. Urgency tangled her words. "No! This is Ruby McClure. Detective Harriman knows me. And he knows Alexis. See, Nick's DNA got on Lucy Hayes's hand because of the paramedics. And now the guy who really killed her has taken Alexis."

"So you're a friend of Nick's?"

"Yes," Ruby said with relief.

"Look, I appreciate you trying to throw a red herring into the mix to help a friend, but I don't have time for this. I'm hanging up now."

And then Ruby was left with nothing but dead air.

NOT PERSONAL

"WHAT?" ALEXIS'S HEART STUTTERED. "WHY do you have to kill me?" She didn't realize she had lifted her foot from the accelerator until he nudged her again with the gun.

"I'm sorry. It's not personal." He said this as if she would find it reassuring. "It's just that I made a mistake and now I have to fix it."

Her hands were slick on the wheel. "And how does killing me fix a mistake? Isn't that just another type of mistake? Like two wrongs don't make a right?"

Instead of answering, he said, "Turn here."

"On Pierson?" she asked. It was a silly exercise. No one was listening. Alexis was alone, except for a man who planned to kill her. She was alone, and it probably wouldn't be long until she was dead.

Still, a part of Alexis was surprised when she began to recognize certain landmarks. With every turn, she became more certain. And then he pointed at a white ranch house and told her to park in the driveway. It was right across the street from the vacant lot where Lucy Hayes had been found.

"Is this your house?"

He didn't answer. She remembered the people lined up along the crime scene tape. He must have been one of them. "So you live across the street from where she was found?" It sort of made sense. "What happened? Did you hear her or see her that night and come outside? Did you try to talk to her? And then something went wrong." Alexis was pulling the words out of the air, but she knew she was right by the way his face first softened and then hardened.

"Get out. And don't run or call for help. I'll be right behind you." He pushed her ahead of him, first out of the pickup and then up the walk. Together, they marched up the steps and in the front door. There was a moment where he released her arm to put the key in the lock, but by the time she realized she should ignore the gun and run, the door was swinging open and he was shoving her inside ahead of him. Her heart was beating so hard she could hear it in her ears.

The house smelled stale and somehow sad. An orange-and-white cat scampered into the living room, then skidded to a stop and did the cat version of a double take at the sight of her. It would have been funny if everything else hadn't been so grim.

"Why me?" Alexis said. "I don't understand." She was scanning the room for something she could use as a weapon. Only she found nothing. A black-and-red afghan lay folded over the end of the couch. Opposite was an old TV that probably weighed more than she did. A box of Kleenex on the coffee table. No fireplace with handy cast-iron tools. She could see partway into the small kitchen, but if there was a block of sharp knives on the counter, she didn't see it.

"Because you have that guy's DNA on you," he said. "That Nick Walker's."

"What? He's not my boyfriend or anything."

"But you are friends. And they said on TV that even a single fingerprint has enough DNA to identify who left it. I know he's their number one suspect. I watched them take the sample." He nodded at the white metal blinds. Two of them were bent back at eye level. "So I need to make sure they keep believing he's the one who killed that girl."

"You mean Lucy Hayes?" How long until Alexis was just like Lucy, lying in the cold and the dark while her life ebbed away?

He nodded. "Yes. Once another girl with that guy's DNA on her turns up dead, they'll lock him up and throw away the key."

It kind of made sense. If you were crazy. His coat flapped open, revealing a tan holster on his belt. A holster, not for a gun, but for a knife. With a horrible certainty, she knew it must be the same knife that had killed Lucy.

"Then you must not know." Alexis was thinking faster than she ever had before in her life. Was she really here, in this house that made her think of her grandmother's, trying to fool a killer? "They arrested Nick two hours ago. If I die, then the *one* person they'll know for sure can't have done it is Nick."

"No." He shook his head. "*No.*"

"Yes! And as soon as a second girl turns up dead, they'll let Nick go and come looking for you."

"So what am I supposed to do? Just turn you loose?" He snorted to show how ridiculous the idea was.

"Yes. Exactly." Alexis nodded.

"I wish I could, but then you'll just go running to the police."

Alexis forced her lips into the shape of a smile. "I won't tell anyone. I promise." She tried to make herself believe her own words when she said them. Tried and failed.

He gave her a skeptical look. "Like I believe that." With the gun, he pointed at the couch. "Stop talking and sit down. I need to think."

She did. There were dozens of cat hairs snagged on the green plaid upholstery. Surely some of them were making their way onto her clothes. Maybe she should point them out. Just one more piece of evidence that would link her to this man. But would he listen? He was pacing back and forth, muttering.

She couldn't just sit here and wait to die. "I have to go to the bathroom." A bathroom would have a window. Or something she could turn into a weapon. Or maybe both.

He stopped in his tracks and regarded her with narrowed eyes. "Really?"

Alexis squirmed, doing a better job at lying this time.

"Leave your purse on the couch," he ordered as she stood up. Then he walked her down the hall. "I'm going to stay right out here. And leave the door open an inch."

Alexis walked straight to the window. It was a narrow band of glass that had been patterned so you couldn't see through it. Even if she managed to break it before he was on her, she didn't think she could squeeze through. As quietly as she could, she opened the door under the sink. She had been hoping for a can of Lysol, or some kind of toxic cleanser she could spray or throw into his eyes, but all she found was a can of Bon Ami, which had big letters proclaiming it hypoallergenic. She eased open a drawer. A cache of Avon makeup, all of it well used. So where was the woman it belonged to?

"Hurry up!" he bellowed from the hall.

She flushed the toilet and ran water in the sink without bothering to wash her hands. Maybe the police would find her DNA here as well one day. She stared at the yellow ceramic fish on the wall. Yellow circles had been attached to the wall above it as if it were blowing bubbles. Only an old lady would put that on the wall.

She threw open the bathroom door and made a run for it. Not for the front door, but for the door at the end of the hall.

"Don't go in there!" He tried to stop her, but she flung open the door.

"Help me!" she cried. "Help me!"

There was no one in the room, just a bed covered with a beautiful corduroy-crazy quilt in shades of purple and royal blue. In the corner sat a dresser topped with a TV. Next to it squatted a green machine that was like a cross between a piece of wheeled luggage and an air conditioner. It looked medical.

The man stopped at the threshold. He still held the gun, but it was no longer pointed at her.

Alexis turned to him. "Whose room is this?"

"My mom's."

"Where is she?" But she knew the answer before he

said it. There was an emptiness here that was far deeper than someone having just left the room for a few hours.

"Gone." He took a deep breath. "She died."

"What happened?" Despite herself, Alexis felt a flash of sympathy.

"She'd been sick my whole life. Since I was younger than you. As a result, I didn't get to have much of a life myself. I couldn't date or anything. I don't even know how to talk to girls."

Alexis held his gaze. "You're talking to me now." And it actually was a conversation, a real conversation. Then she added, "Is this what she would want for you?" and broke the spell.

He raised one shoulder. "If it was a choice between me and you, Mom would say I should be the one to live. Sometimes we have to do things we don't want to do. Even if they're hard."

"But not this." She tried to catch his eye again, but he was no longer looking at her directly. "Not stabbing me and putting my body in that vacant lot."

"So you think that if I do that, the cops will know that Nick guy couldn't have done it," he said.

"That's right," Alexis said encouragingly. She was finally getting through to him.

"Then I guess I'll have to put it someplace they can't find it."

DON'T BRING A KNIFE
TO A GUNFIGHT

WHEN RUBY STARTED RUNNING OUT OF the store, Nick was right on her heels. Ignoring the stares of the shoppers, he concentrated on trying to hear the clues Alexis was giving.

"That Detective Meeker didn't believe me," Ruby said as they raced back to her car. "It's up to us to save Alexis."

Nick put his hand over the phone, just in case whoever was with Alexis could hear him. "Alexis just said something about him living across the street from where they found Lucy's body."

"That fits the profile," Ruby said between gasps, "of the unplanned killer! Acting in his own neighborhood."

As they threw themselves into her car, Nick reached into his pocket, feeling for the one thing that might make a difference. He just feared they were going to be too late.

Ruby started to say something more, but Nick held up his hand to tell her to be quiet. On the phone, he heard the man who had taken Alexis shouting. But he couldn't make out the words. And he couldn't hear Alexis at all anymore. For a minute, he was overwhelmed by thoughts of her: of her silver-blue eyes, of her kindness, of the easy way she moved. The world needed Alexis in it.

Ruby sped down Broadway, jumping from lane to lane whenever the one they were in slowed down. Within seconds, they were on the freeway.

In Nick's hand, Ruby's phone had gone silent. He held his breath, his finger in his other ear, and listened as hard as he could, ignoring the buzzing starting to come from his pocket.

Nothing.

Did that mean Alexis might already be dead?

"I can't hear anything anymore," he told Ruby. His bones felt like water. In answer, she pushed the accelerator down even farther.

It was only when they neared the vacant lot that she started driving slower. Which house could it be?

Then Nick spotted an old blue Chevy pickup with a silver grille. He remembered Kyle saying that a truck like that had passed him that night as he walked home from the Last Exit.

"There!" he said, pointing. "I think that's it." He was out of the car before Ruby had even brought it to a complete stop and running across the lawn. Acting without thought. All he knew was that he had to save Alexis before it was too late. He rang the bell. Did he hear shouting inside? His heart was racing and his mouth was dry.

He pulled the Kershaw from his pocket and pressed the button. In a split second the blade was out and gleaming. Folded, the knife was no longer than the palm of his hand. That was what Nick liked about it. But now he realized he was going to have to get really close to do any damage. Close enough that he himself could easily get hurt. With his free hand, he pounded on the door. "Alexis!" he shouted. "Are you in there?"

Ruby joined him on the front steps. When she saw the knife, she did a double take.

A man in his midthirties flung open the door. He wore an ill-fitting suit. Nick remembered him standing along the crime scene tape, near him and Kyle. But what really struck Nick was that even though he was inside, the man was wearing gloves. Or at least that he was wearing one on his left hand, the hand Nick could see.

"What do you want?" he snarled. He barely glanced at Nick's knife.

"We're here for our friend Alexis. And don't try to stop us!" Wishing that his voice was deeper, Nick brandished the knife. Wishing that he was bigger. This guy wasn't that much taller than him, but he looked strong, with a thick neck and shoulders. Nick could really use some backup right about now, but all he had was a girl who was even skinner and shorter than him.

"Alexis?" Ruby shouted. "Alexis, are you in there?"

No answer. Was she already dead, the way the man on the telephone had threatened? Nick uttered a silent prayer that was only a single word. *Please, please, please, please.*

"I don't know what your deal is or who you're talking about!" the man snarled. "All I know is you had better get off my porch now."

Somewhere in the recesses of the house, Nick heard a thump.

Ruby ducked under the man's arm and ran in.

"Alexis!" she shouted. "Alexis?"

The man ran after her, and Nick followed the man. He stared at his back, trying to think of the best place to stab him. It was all fine when it was a movie or a video game, but when you were looking at your four-inch blade and wondering just how far it would get inside someone and how gross it would be, it was something else.

Ruby pointed at the couch, her face triumphant. "What do you call that? That is Alexis's purse."

"And what do you call this?" Now Nick saw what was in the man's other hand. It was a gun. *What was that saying?* he thought. *Don't bring a knife to a gunfight?*

But what choice did he have? Nick raised his knife and prepared to charge.

The sound of the shot filled the room. Something slapped his hand away. Nick didn't have the knife anymore. And his hand was bleeding. A lot.

He had been shot.

He fell to his knees. The world spun as if he were on a Tilt-A-Whirl. The bitter taste of bile filled his mouth. He started to slump sideways. He couldn't stop staring at the raw meat that used to be the base of his thumb. It had been bad enough when it was Lucy's blood he had crawled through, Mariana's blood glowing in his headlamp. This—this was his own blood. His lifeblood.

No. He could not pass out. Remembering Ruby's advice, Nick forced every muscle to go rigid, ignoring the fact that it seemed to make the blood pulse from the wound even faster.

In the background, Ruby was screaming.

What was that glinting on the floor in front of him? The knife! Only a few feet away. He lunged for it.

The guy laughed and kicked it away. Nick landed on his hands. A scream was ripped from his mouth. The pain was like nothing he had ever experienced. It felt like he had just tried to pick up a snapped power line. Pulsing, burning agony raced from his bleeding hand up into his shoulder and then engulfed his entire body.

He slumped to the floor, closed his eyes, and let in the darkness.

"Nick?" Ruby said. "Nick?" She sounded frantic. "He's going to bleed to death."

"I'm sorry, but you're all going to die," the guy said as he stepped over Nick.

Nick lay curled in a fetal position. His bad hand was right next to one of his feet. Beside the shoe that had the razor blade tucked in the insole. What good would an inch-long blade do him? Better to lie here. Better to surrender to the peace.

But did he hear something in the distance? Was it a siren? In the car he had turned on his phone, hoping that Ruby was right. Hoping that the police were monitoring its location. Now they might be coming. Maybe. But even if they were, Nick was afraid it was too late. Too late for everyone.

In his mind's eye, he saw the faces of Alexis and Ruby. If he was going to die, it was better to die for something. And while it might be too late for Alexis, it wasn't for Ruby.

He just wished he had kissed Alexis. Even once.

Nick tensed every muscle. Pushed his teeth into his tongue. At the same time, he slid his index finger into his shoe, curling it under the insole. He knew he had found the razor blade when he felt it slice into his finger. Undeterred, he hooked it out.

He gripped the single-edged blade between his finger and thumb. He was so weak he wasn't even sure he had it the right way around. His fingers were slippery with blood.

The man was standing sideways to him. Nick pushed on the floor with his good hand and launched himself at him, slashing the razor blade at ankle level.

The blade caught and held. And then it felt like a guitar string snapping. The pressure was suddenly gone. Screaming, the guy pitched sideways.

But he was still holding the gun. He propped himself on one elbow and took aim. And now the gun's round, empty eye focused on Nick.

The second shot rang out just as the door went flying backward and Harriman barreled in.

And then the world went dark.

CHAPTER 50

NICK

TUESDAY

I OWE YOU

WHEN NICK WOKE UP, HIS THOUGHTS FELT fuzzy and slow. Above him was a white acoustical tile ceiling. And underneath him was what he thought was some kind of bed. In the background, a lot of beeping, overhead pages, and muffled conversations.

Slowly, it came to him. He was in a hospital.

And he was there because he had been shot.

It took a great deal of effort to move his head, but he finally managed to look down at his hand. It was wrapped in thick white bandages. But at least he still had a hand. Panic jolted him a bit more awake. What if he didn't have all his fingers? He raised his hand toward his face—it seemed to weigh twenty pounds—and tried to count the pink tips protruding from the layers.

"So you're awake now?" It was Ruby's voice.

Five. At least, he thought there were five. Nick managed to turn his head.

Alexis and Ruby were sitting beside his bed. "My hand?" he asked.

"They said you were really lucky. The gunshot just grazed you. You had to have some stitches on it and where you cut your fingers on that razor blade, but they said you'll be okay." Alexis's eyes sparkled with unshed tears. "Your mom and brother just went to eat in the cafeteria. We told them we'd give them a break."

Ruby got to her feet and pushed her chair back. "I'll go tell Harriman you're awake now. He wants to talk to you. They've been interviewing that guy. Kenny Moxley. They shot him before he could kill you. But don't worry, he's on another floor with a police guard."

After she left, Alexis leaned so close that Nick could smell her breath. It smelled like coffee and cinnamon.

It was the best thing Nick had ever smelled.

"I owe you," Alexis said in a low voice. "I thought I was dead for sure. He had tied me up and gagged me. Even though he kept saying he was sorry, he was planning on killing me as soon as it was dark. But you saved me."

"I didn't save you." His tongue was like a piece of leather in his mouth. "The police did."

"But you're the one who turned on your phone so they would track you down." Alexis sat on the side of the bed. It dipped slightly under her weight. "And you're the one who was willing to fight back with nothing more than a razor blade. If you hadn't done that . . ." Letting the words trail off, she leaned over and gave him a hug, tucking her head next to his.

Suddenly Nick felt completely awake. Alexis's ribs were pressing painfully on his injured hand, squishing it against his stomach, but he didn't complain. He didn't even try to pull it free.

When she started to straighten up, he put his good hand on the back of her neck and pulled her back down. For a second, her soft lips landed on his. Then she pulled her head back and stood up.

"What was that?"

"I'm sorry," Nick said. But he wasn't.

Alexis closed her eyes and ran her fingertips across her lips. But it wasn't like she was wiping him away. More like she was exploring. Remembering. At least that's how it seemed to him.

She opened her eyes. "Look. We're friends, Nick. Friends. But that's all. I'm sorry."

"Of course." He put on a smile. "I guess I'm still a little loopy from the anesthesia."

"Somebody tells me you're awake," Harriman called from the door.

"More or less," Nick said. He and Alexis exchanged a glance. He wondered how much Harriman had heard.

"I've already done my interview, Nick, so I'm going to go." Alexis nodded at him and left. He knew he should feel embarrassed or maybe sad for how things had gone, but he kept thinking, *I kissed Alexis Frost.*

Harriman closed the door and then took the chair Alexis had just been sitting in. "I owe you an apology. We made a mistake." He hesitated. "*I* made a mistake. I'm sorry."

Nick started to cross his arms but thought better of trying to bend his damaged hand. "You thought I did it."

"When you're a cop, there are a lot of things you wish weren't true that are. This was one of them. But I should have gone with my gut. Because my gut said you didn't do it." He pressed his lips together so hard that the skin around them went white.

"Maybe next time you'll listen to your gut." Nick wasn't quite ready to forgive, but he could see how much the other man was struggling. And the memory of Alexis's kiss softened him.

"Technology's only as good as the human beings interpreting it. We screwed up. And almost got you kids killed."

Nick didn't like being called a kid, but it didn't seem worth arguing over. He sniffed. Could he still smell that coffee/cinnamon scent lingering in the air? And did Alexis always smell like that?

"It should have been a clue that the only DNA we got off the brick was Lucy's. Finding your DNA on her hand but not on the brick didn't add up, but we didn't even try to account for it. It starts to make sense if you know Moxley was wearing gloves."

"What about Lucy's hand?"

"Even though we can find DNA, it still can't tell you exactly when it was deposited or under what circumstances. In fact, the crime lab doesn't even test for the source, whether it's skin or blood or whatever. They just look for DNA. And spit—which, it turns out, is a big part of vomit—is an even better DNA source than blood. From what Ruby tells me, some of yours must have ended up on that accident victim when you held her hand. And that DNA got transferred to the pulse oximeter and then transferred to Lucy when the paramedics responded to the call about her being found in the vacant lot. It's called secondary transfer."

Nick didn't even feel embarrassed by the whole vomiting thing anymore. "Ruby's the one who figured it out."

"Yeah, that Ruby." Harriman shook his head. "Who knows how her mind works."

"I think it works pretty well," Nick said sharply.

Harriman held up a hand. "I wasn't dissing her. She's pretty amazing, actually. If she didn't have a different way of looking at things, this all could have gone a lot worse." He rummaged in his coat pocket and took out a tape recorder. "Now I need to talk to you about what happened in Kenny Moxley's house."

Nick started with seeing Kenny at the SAR search. When he got to the part about Moxley shooting the knife from his hand, Harriman said, "If you're holding a weapon, that's where people tend to shoot, because it's what they're staring at. Even in gunfights between people who are familiar with firearms, both will tend to shoot at each other's hands. And you were the first—and we believe only—person Moxley ever shot."

Nick started to say something more, but all he could do was yawn.

Harriman clicked off his tape recorder. "I think I should let you get some rest."

After he left, Nick curled on his side, holding his injured hand off the bed, suspended in space. He wondered if his dad knew what had happened. A part of him even wondered if his dad was proud of him.

His dreams had all been based on lies.

The truth was a lot more complicated. Everything had changed.

Nick still had so many things to decide. Who he was. Who he took after. Who he wanted to be.

But for now he was going to sleep.

CHAPTER 51

NICK

SATURDAY

EVEN IF

NICK'S MOCHA SAT UNTOUCHED AS HE waited for Alexis to walk through the doors of Stumptown Coffee. Ruby was coming, too, but it was the thought of Alexis that had tied Nick's stomach in knots. He couldn't bring himself to take a single sip, despite the lines of chocolate zigzagging over the whipped cream.

Remembering how Alexis always carefully counted her money, Nick had gotten her one, too. She deserved more than a house coffee. After a moment's hesitation, he had ordered one for Ruby as well.

Since he still couldn't use his right hand, Nick had had to make three trips to carry everything to the table. The doctor had told him that if the bullet had nicked one-sixteenth of an inch deeper, it would have hit bones or tendons. The way the doctor had described it, Nick was extremely lucky, even if he had lost a lot of blood from both the bullet and the razor blade. Maybe seeing all that blood would finally help desensitize him.

A tall blond girl walked in, loosening the wool around

her neck. But it wasn't Alexis. When she finally did come in, should he hug her? Kiss her cheek? Tell her how pretty she looked? Because even though he hadn't seen her yet, he knew Alexis would look amazing.

Today was Saturday, and it would be the first time they had seen each other since he had kissed her in the hospital. Or, as Nick liked to think of it, since *they* had kissed. Because he was certain there had been a moment when she had returned his kiss. Pretty certain, anyway.

Had she told Bran about what had happened between them? What did she think of Nick now? Could she possibly be interested in him as more than a friend?

The last few days had been a blur. On Thursday, he had gone back to school, graciously accepted the principal's apology. Everywhere he went, kids and even teachers wanted to hear more about what had happened. Yesterday, a TV crew had interviewed him right in front of school. One of the crew had tried to shoo away the onlookers, without much success, not that Nick minded. People who had never even noticed him before were now saying hi in the hall like they had always been friends. Especially girls. But always hovering in the back of his thoughts was the memory of Alexis and that moment in the hospital when he had pulled her close.

And here she was, pushing her blond curls out of her eyes as she walked in with Ruby. They were deep in conversation about something that had made even Ruby put on the smallest of smiles. Were they talking about him?

He waved. "Over here, guys. I already got your stuff. My treat."

Ruby stopped short even as Alexis took a seat. "Why are you wearing a tie?" she demanded.

Nick looked down. The tie was yellow with tiny navy-blue dots. He had borrowed it from Kyle's closet. It made him look older. Not that he was going to tell Ruby that. "I had another interview this morning. With KATU."

"Did you allow that tie to touch any of our cups?"

"What?" He looked at Alexis, but she seemed just as confused as he was.

"Nobody ever washes their ties. And they brush against all kinds of viruses and bacteria and just plain dirt." Ruby made a face. "If I go to a doctor and he's wearing one, I ask him to take it off and then wash his hands."

Understanding dawned. "Because it could transfer germs from a sick person to you," Nick said. "Just like that pulse oximeter transferred my DNA to Lucy."

"Otherwise known as a pulse ox," Ruby said. "Exactly."

"Don't worry. It didn't come anywhere near your drinks," Nick said, although he really had no idea. Ruby finally sat down but didn't reach for her coffee. Alexis had already picked hers up, and now she took a sip and gave Nick a grateful smile. With that smile, all the knots in his stomach loosened, and he picked his up, too.

Then she said, "Thank you. And Bran and I saw you on Channel 8 last night. You looked good."

The knots retied themselves. He set his coffee back down, untouched. "I made sure I didn't mention either of your names." For their own reasons, each girl wanted to fly under the radar. "The reporter told me they're saying the surgery to repair that guy's Achilles tendon was successful, although he'll probably always have a limp."

"I still don't understand why you had a razor blade in your shoe." Ruby's brows pulled together.

How could Nick explain it to them? "Everyone but you guys thought I killed Lucy. My dad even told me that he would look out for me in prison." He remembered the clang of the doors, the guard's stare, the smell of sewage and sweat, his father's dead eyes. A shiver ran through him, hard enough that his untouched coffee slopped over the edge of the mug. "Just being there to visit that one time was enough. I knew I couldn't face going to prison."

Alexis got it right away. She touched the back of one hand with a fingertip. Her nails were bitten to the quick, which made him forgive her instantly, made him love her even more. "Oh, Nick, you wouldn't have, would you?"

"I don't know. I don't think so. It was just a weird kind of comfort when I was desperate, you know?"

Ruby still looked a little bit lost, but Alexis nodded. "Are you going to see your dad again?" she asked. He could still feel the brush of her finger.

"I don't know."

"Still," Alexis said, "he is your dad."

Unexpectedly, her words stung. Maybe Nick could forgive his dad for what he had done, but that didn't mean he had to actually let him into his life after all these years. "Your dad isn't in your life, though, right? And you don't seem to mind."

"That's different." Alexis's mouth twisted.

"How?"

"I don't really want to talk about it."

He made himself pull back. "I guess my mom still goes to see my dad sometimes because she still remembers the person he used to be. Same with my brother, but since he doesn't remember as much, he doesn't go as often. And I don't have any memories of who he was before. Not really." It still felt weird knowing just what a huge secret they had kept from him for years and years. He understood their reasons, but he didn't agree with them.

A silence fell over the table.

"Have you heard what Dimitri has been calling us?" Ruby said. "The three musketeers."

In her clumsy way, she was trying to change the subject, trying to save Alexis and Nick from feeling the pain she saw but didn't understand.

Still, Nick liked the sound of it. He raised his mug. "To us. The three musketeers."

They clinked mugs and smiled at each other. Friends.

Maybe that wasn't everything Nick wanted, but for today it was enough. As he looked from Ruby to Alexis, he put his mug to his lips and drank in the sweetness.

ACKNOWLEDGMENTS

A lot of *Blood Will Tell* revolves around DNA and its implications. DNA expert Daniel Krane, PhD, research scientist and professor at Wright State University and founder of Forensic Bioinformatics, graciously answered question after question. As I was revising the book, Nathaniel David Adams, a bioinformatician who works with Dan and who was also once an EMT, helped me get all the details right.

I met Dan through Lee Lofland, a veteran police investigator and founder of the one and only Writers' Police Academy, where Dan was a featured speaker in 2013. The Crime Scene Questions for Writers group on Yahoo was also a wonderful place to gather accurate information. And Robin Burcell, a former cop and author in her own right, helped me with information about questioning juveniles.

As for Portland County Sheriff's Office Search and Rescue, it was modeled on the real-life Multnomah County Sheriff's Office Search and Rescue (MCSO SAR). Not only does the group find people lost outdoors, but it also searches for crime scene evidence and recovers human remains. Jake Keller has volunteered with MCSO SAR since he was a teen, and he has patiently answered dozens of questions, including questions about knives.

Speaking of knives, thanks to the customer service folks at Global Restaurant Solutions and to the produce staff at both New Seasons and Food Front for not getting freaked out about my questions.

Kudo to my editor, Christy Ottaviano, for championing Nick, Alexis, and Ruby. Other wonderful folks at Henry Holt include Amy Allen, April Ward, Holly Hunnicutt, Allison Verost, Ksenia Winnicki, Marianne Cohen, Christine Ma, Angus Killick, Katie Fee, and Lucy Del Priore.

And this past year, my agent, Wendy Schmalz, and I marked our twentieth anniversary of being a team.